come
to
africa
and
save
your
marriage

and other stories

also by Maria Thomas

Antonia Saw the Oryx First

come
to
africa
and
save
your
marriage

and other stories

Maria Thomas

The following stories have been previously published, some of them in different form: "Why the Sky Is So Far Away," "A Thief in My House" and "The Texan" in *StoryQuarterly*; "Summer Opportunity" and "Silver Sugar from Bombay" in *North American Review*; and "Jim Chance" in *The Antioch Review* as "Charlie Speed"; and "She Hears, Falling, the Seed" in *Arrival* magazine.

Published in the United States of America by
Soho Press, Inc.,
1 Union Square,
New York, N.Y. 10003.

Library of Congress Cataloging-in-Publication Data

Thomas, Maria, 1941–
    Come to Africa and save your marriage and other stories.

    1. Americans—Africa—Fiction.   2. Africa—
Fiction.   I. Title.
PS3570.H5735C6   1987   813.'54   87-9786
ISBN 0–939149–06–0

Manufactured in the United States of America

First Edition

To my main men,
Thomas J. and Raphael D. Worrick

With special thanks to
Nat Sobel

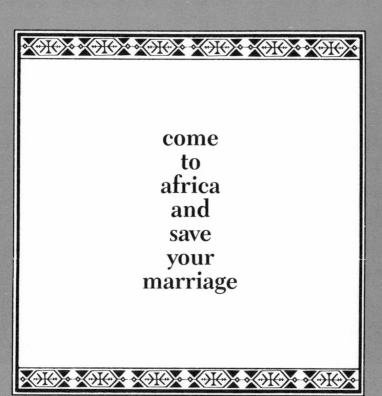

come
to
africa
and
save
your
marriage

Things in the tropics have different proportions, like the vegetation, intense and overgrown. Like Rashak, his eyes deep set with long, dark lashes, his nose thin, arched, aristocratic, a bird of prey. High cheekbones and deep olive skin, and his lush hair, copper in the sun, curled below his ears. If I had been Lewis Rashak's wife—me, Marlene—and someone else as well, someone on the outside looking in, I might have seen the humor in it all. Lewis liked to stage our lives—producer, director, playwright—our little, in-the-kitchen-one-acts with no audience, but the players, me and the kids, and then, finally, Marie D'Avignon.

Lewis fell in love with Marie. He told me, rather "had to tell me," as soon as they became lovers, a confession made all the more dramatic by the understated way we played it, seeing who was more mature.

I said, "Well, it's okay, it happens, but aren't you ratting on Marie, my best friend?"

"She isn't happy about that part of it," he said.

She was outside, in fact, waiting while he told me, sitting on her motorcycle staring into her helmet the way she did. I went to her and said, "It's okay, Marie. Don't feel bad for me or anything. I mean it." I even hugged her, but she didn't look convinced. She was almost crying. She knew, of course, the way things were with Rashak and me.

Rashak was standing in the kitchen door with his back to us. A chair had blocked the entrance. Behind him you could see the filthy stove, the piled dishes, the soot from the charcoal we sometimes cooked on to save on the electric bill. When he heard us come in, he kicked over the chair and went into the kitchen. Marie followed him and I stepped away from them, down into the living room. I did the only thing I could, tidied aimlessly, but there was so much junk—the furniture had become obsolete, turned into storage space. In the corner was my "workshop," four orange crates, a coffee cup, the buckets of dried clay, the broken pots, and the headless dancer modeled from Hanna, my older daughter.

Hanna broke the silence. "Mommy! Daddy!" rushing toward the door shouting about a snake in the neighbors' yard. Jenny, the younger one, was hopping barefoot behind him over the stones.

"It was a co-brass," she shouted. "And its head went uuuup like this!"

"And its tongue went like thiiiiis." Hanna dashed—I saw it coming, but too late—her hand right through the screen.

"Goddamn it!" Rashak yelled from the kitchen. "I just taped that fucking screen. Christ, there are flies all over the place in here. We're lucky we don't all have cholera."

"What about the three windows that have fallen out upstairs?" Me, nagging from the other room. "Why don't you bother to fix those if you don't like flies?"

Marie had slipped to the dining room, so quietly I barely noticed. She sat at the table there. She drew Jenny to her lap. There were crayons and papers around, spread out from another time, so the two of them started to make pictures. Lewis grabbed a cup from the table and went back to the kitchen.

"Would you like some *instant*, Marie? Marlene, you? We only have *instant*." This was sarcasm; he hated instant coffee. "One more cup of this stuff and I'll puke," he said. He tipped the cup, dribbling the residue over the floor. "Isn't there ever anything else to drink in this place?" "There's tea," I told him. He hated tea.

Living with Lewis Rashak was never a joke. His mother had been in show biz, a comedienne on the Catskill circuit. She had been a friend of Lenny Bruce. From her, Lewis picked up the habit of keeping oddballs around the house. At that time it was Ramji Gupta, an Indian mathematician and poet, his wife Ingrid who was Swedish and made documentary films, and their huge baby whose name I can't remember. The University of Dar es Salaam had terminated Gupta's contract some seven months early for no reason and had put them out of their house. They had no place to go and were camping, to protest the broken contract, on the front lawn of their former house under canopies of faded cloths. Ingrid filmed their struggle and Ramji had written a long, satiric narrative poem about it which he jokingly compared to the *Ramayana*. But Gupta was far too skinny to clown around and no one ever laughed at his jokes.

When it had started to rain, Lewis took pity on them and invited them to fold up their tents and come stay at our place. They camped in our living room and the only compensation was Gupta's vegetarian food.

I hated it in Africa when we first came. We had no money, were already threadbare, and Lewis's salary as an instructor in the English department was an African salary, meant for people who can live on nothing. Everything had to be makeshift, permanently temporary. I couldn't do my pottery. I couldn't buy bricks for a kiln, or wood to fire it. I couldn't afford glazes. There was plenty of clay in the river and I tried to build a kiln of sundried brick. First I made the bricks and then I dug the foundation. Then the rains came. The bricks dissolved. Nothing remained. It was the first thing I learned about the tropics. The few pots I made went unfired, piled in the living room—the so-called living room—so brittle they were turning to dust: red dust on the books, on Rashak's desk, on the torn seat covers, the bare floor, the dying house plants. But in the end, I was glad I came, because I fell in love, too, though I hadn't told Lewis. When I did tell him, I wanted to be ready to stand back and watch the scene, outside myself, so I could laugh.

What I told him first was that I wanted out. "Move Marie over here and I'll live at her place." I knew he couldn't afford it. There were the kids and no way for me to get a job, an alien with no working papers.

He turned around and told Ingrid, "Marlene wants to split. She blames me for holding her back. She resents my work. All that shit."

Ingrid said, "Vomen need her independence." Her baby crawled out from under the table with Jenny's Fisher-Price truck.

"Was it Lewis's work that I had to hire out for odd jobs so his kids could eat while he played around for years writing some useless Ph.D. on African Literature, for God's sake? So he could get ahead? Ahead, my ass. What about *my* work, Rashak?"

"Oh, yes," he said, "those dessicating lumps of clay. She calls that dust in there 'her work.'"

Jenny was screaming, "*It's my truck!*" She had started to pummel the baby. There was so much yelling at times it hurt, physical pain, as though you'd been hit, across your back, across your chest.

"The Masai tribe make successes in marriage," Ingrid said, "by having absolutely nothing to do with each other but sex." She was serious. Her round red face, bright yellow hair, chapped and peeling lips, seemed suspended in the room like a Cheshire cat. The baby was quiet now, climbing the table, trying to stand up on it.

You should have seen how he came coaxing later; Rashak's style, an arrangement. "Look, Marlene, can't we just go on the way we were? Stay friends. We're mature adults, after all."

"So are you going to sleep with the two of us tag-team style?"

"Shit, Marlene," he said, "you know I can't do that. I'm a one-woman man." He meant one woman at a time, and of course that was Marie. We were all too close. *She* must have insisted.

"What am I supposed to do in the meantime?" I moved my hips to show him what.

"Take a lover," he said. I wanted to tell him right then, "I have a lover." But I was waiting.

The next Saturday night Ramji made his specialty for dinner, curried eggs, dhal, chapattis, green mango pickle, coconut chutney. Rashak had produced a bottle of red wine somehow and Marie brought brandy for after. The table was cleared and set, a miracle. There were even napkins and candles. Lewis was all prim in ironed jeans and a crisp blue shirt. I smelled his after-shave lotion. In the candlelight the place had a new look, as though new people had moved in. It lightened Rashak who could flit around like an insect.

But new people had not moved in. Gupta's baby, who didn't wear diapers, had climbed onto the table and managed to shit in one of the plates. Ingrid, laughing and talking Swedish, hauled him off. It was something I couldn't resist, giggling, carrying the plate, offering it to Lewis as an *hors d'oeuvre.* He didn't think it was funny, reeled with disgust, and grabbed the plate. For a minute I thought he would throw it at me, but he resisted, storming away from us. Marie flushed and followed him. She carried him a beer. His lover.

The food was good, the ambiance at the meal not so good. A paper plate thrown by Hanna landed in the egg curry and Jenny's braid caught fire as she leaned across a candle to grab a chapatti. She tried the mango pickle after Lewis warned her not to and then spit most of it into his plate.

"Why must we always have the *kids*?" he wanted to know.

Ingrid and Ramji talked steadily about how the United States was using wheat-crop politics to enslave the world, holding entire continents hostage to famine. Ingrid had read somewhere that the earth's poles were shifting and there would be drastic changes in the weather by the year two thousand. By an ironic twist of nature, only Canada, the United States, and Australia would be able to produce enough grain. They would try to suppress the world. But nature, Ingrid explained, was more than shifting winds and currents. Masses of starving dark people would rise up and take everything. They were out there right now, she warned, having more and more babies despite America's attempt to impose genocidal policies of population control. As a statement, Ingrid, herself, was planning to have ten children.

Later they were surprised when I said, "I'm going out for a walk."

"But is it safe?" Gupta asked.

"I'm coming with you," Rashak announced. Marie rose with him.

"Hey, I want to be alone. Understand?" They let me go, but I heard Lewis whisper to the others as I closed the screen door, "Marlene's taking it hard."

Truth was that I went to meet John Mwema, as we had planned, down behind the Danish couple's, at the bridge, just below where I tried to build my kiln, so that if they had looked from our living-room window, Rashak and the others, they would have seen me run to him and all the joy of it, lifting there, racing, laughing, and taking the hill, down to where we went. Mwema was one of Rashak's English students. A gifted poet. Rashak always talked him up—Mwema this, Mwema that—and had him to our house so much it just grew until there were no surprises in the end except how good it felt. So good it made me wonder what had ever gone on between me and Rashak that I had thought was love.

Mwema wasn't experienced with women—his marriage had been arranged; his wife, a stranger who stayed in a village far away—and he knew nothing about the world I came from. It made him seem shy when he wasn't, made him seem dull when he wasn't. But as I watched him discover the ability to write, I learned the truth about him. Rashak couldn't coach him, couldn't direct him; it was all there, ready-made, as if he had been born to feel everything and reflect it. Seeing a soul uncover itself that way was, for me, like finding a new fruit. Taste it. Taste it—like that—all you wanted to do. And we were luscious, we were sweet and juicy, even as it rained that first time, there on the beach, covered with sand, rolling in the storm. The bricks dissolved. Nothing remained. And it stayed like this for us all the times we were together.

When I got home that night, everything was dark and the doors were locked. I figured it was Lewis's revenge, so I climbed the grillwork behind the kitchen to the bathroom window. When I tried to open it, the flimsy frame broke and the damn thing clattered to the ground. The Gupta kid cried out somewhere downstairs and a knife or fork fell. I was able to get in, and sat on the can trying to fix the curtain so it would stop the mosquitoes. When I finally wandered into bed, Rashak wasn't there.

Next morning, Ingrid and Ramji, as usual, were sprawled under their cloths on the floor. Their baby had crawled up to his favorite place on the table and gone to sleep with his head in a greasy plate. Our tiny house couldn't take it. The bathroom looked like the facility at the train station in Naples; the kitchen like a war zone. Ingrid woke up and we sat drinking instant coffee in what was left of the cool air from the night before. Maybe it was my guilt. I wanted to make excuses, I bitched about Rashak, telling the old story, because I wanted to tell everyone again and again. How I had worked at a dumb job while Lewis went to school, gave up everything. How Lewis made it seem as though it was for *us*, even bringing us to Africa, an attempt to save the marriage, a once-in-a-lifetime adventure, a chance to experience, to start over.

Ingrid gave her usual advice, "Marlene, you look too much to Lewis. Look to yourself."

Then Jenny came awake, found no one in our bed, and panicked, screaming. Before I could get there, Hanna had clobbered her, shouting, "She *woked* me up!" over and over again, as Jenny howled. The racket woke up Ingrid's baby and the whole place crumbled with noise. Lewis, arriving on Marie's bike, made it worse, shouting that I had abandoned the kids. He pounded on the table, said I was deliberately ruining his life. He couldn't think, couldn't work. I wanted him to fail. And it was all so cheap.

"Where were you last night?" he asked. "You saw her." He grabbed at Ingrid, wanting to drag her into the fight. "She just walked out of here for no reason. Where did she go?"

"I spent the night in my own bed," I answered. "I didn't see you there."

"You're jealous," he said. "I won't put up with that jealous shit."

When he finally stopped, it was as though someone had stopped air-hammering the sidewalk next door—the noise, and the effort, the work just tolerating the sound and then the blessed quiet, the dust and the rubble of blasted cement.

Some of Rashak's students threw a party at a house they had rented in Mikorosheni village. Down there, people fried things all night. There was no electricity and their charcoal fires and kerosene lanterns were the only lights, gathered under makeshift stalls, the midnight snackbars of the tropics. We collected goodies as we went, piled in Joe Ithana's car. There wasn't a road, only random open spaces between mud houses and battered palm trees. There was no moon that night and, black on their black verandas, people were all but invisible. Eyes, and the flash of pale cloths. A white T-shirt. I knew Mwema would be there and had decided that this was it, I was going to leave with him, or stay with him, whatever I had to do to make it clear. I thought, if I could stand outside myself and watch this, how it would make me laugh.

If I could see myself, even now—cozy with John Mwema in a corner near a candle. Something that sounds like a band starts and stops in another room, out of which tumble four or five radical sisters in battle fatigues. Ezekiel Mzizi is asking me about black theater in the States. He thinks that, since he's a good actor, he ought to go to New York. All night there are attempts at music but these fail and at two o'clock or so the party starts to droop around the edges. If I could see it, even now, as a pantomime: me, bleary, propped by Mwema on one elbow and a bookcase on the other. Lewis is in front of us, touching my hand, smiling, lips moving. He takes my shoulders and kisses me on the mouth, a brotherly little thing, but I say something that makes him stiffen. Mwema shrugs. Lewis speaks again, raises his hand. I think he's going to hit me but instead he spreads his fingers through his hair, talking and talking. I'm just laughing there, shaking my head.

And if I were going to do the dialogue for the scene, we'd hear Lewis say, "Time to go now, Marlene." The brotherly kiss now, me balancing against a bookcase, teetering away.

I say, "Well, I think I'll stay here with Mwema tonight." A little drunk. Lewis is stymied, staring so you think he's missed everything.

He says, "Marlene, I want you to leave this place with me. After that you can do what you want."

"I'm going to do what I want right now." At which point he raises his hand, reconsiders, fans open his fingers, combs his hair. There's no chance for his script in this theater, not with this audience, and not with the cast of characters he's got to work with—the tall, handsome African, the white wife, the cuckold husband.

Lewis didn't speak to me when I got home the next day. He'd gone on a house-cleaning binge. Ingrid, in a panic that he would kick them out, had folded her bedding and put the cushions back on the couch. I could see Ramji meditating in the yard. Jennifer, who had been prompted to play the neglected child, hurled herself at me, weeping, "Mommy! Mommy! Daddy said you were lost!"

"Did you? Did you tell her that, you bastard? Daddy knows I wasn't lost, Jenny. Daddy knows where I was." Rashak didn't respond. The silent treatment. He sulked at his desk, fixed his own food, and talked to Ingrid at long intervals and in whispers. But I knew that Lewis Rashak couldn't keep silent for long.

That night we ended up in the same bed. Lewis stripped completely and sat on the edge of it to smoke a cigarette. My back was toward him.

"At first Marie and I only kissed," he said. "For a long time. Just kissed. Because she was being true to *you!*" He laughed. "But it grew in intensity. I felt her tongue tentatively on my lips. She was shy; she told me there had only been two others. So I licked her tongue gently with my own. She was frightened, but she wanted more. She stopped wearing a bra, did you notice, so I could . . ."

I covered my ears with a pillow. "Jealous shit!" he shouted. His voice seemed to have changed. I didn't recognize it. "You listen to me!" He grabbed me hard by the neck and threw the pillow on the floor.

"You pervert!" I was crying now and afraid of him. I had never been afraid of him before.

"Sometimes if she wore a blouse," he went on, "or that red print dress with the buttons, she would let me unfasten it. She has beautiful breasts. But I had to move slowly with her. She was like a virgin . . ."

I tried not to hear it but his words beat into my ears, how he touched Marie, kissed her breasts, stroked her until she came, how she would moan, touch him, but she wouldn't let him screw her until one day, in a display of lust, he took her, weeping. They were both weeping. I thought: For God's sake, he raped her, raped her and is proud.

When he finished his story, he was breathing hard and I was scared he would want sex with me. I kept still, my back toward him. "Now you tell me." He pulled my arm, twisting me to look at him, his eyes so deep in their sockets they seemed to have disappeared. "Start by telling me how long you and the African have been cheating on me." I didn't move. I stayed there curled like a fetus. "Marlene, we can never get anywhere if you don't tell me." He touched me gently then. "Listen, you have humiliated me. When I said to take a lover, I did not mean one of my students. I did not mean an African."

I could hear him fumbling with some paper, rolling a joint. The smell of the match, the sulfur, the sharp perfume of the grass. He shook me, offering to share it. I rolled up, hunched over my knees. "Marlene, Marlene, when I visualize you two together, it revolts me." I sucked in the smoke, held my breath. "Marlene, I forbid you to continue this affair. You probably have a disease."

The grass was strong. Three pulls and the front of my brain opened up. I could see three hundred and sixty degrees through the round window of my skull. Lewis, garish, hair bright red, two dimensional, a cutout, pasted on the slick front of a rock album. Lewis then, like an animated drawing, pulling the straps of my nightgown, pressing down on me, pressing flat; and out the top of my head, a disk rimmed with eyes, I saw the walls, peeling paint, torn curtains, piles of books, dirty coffee mugs, black sky, and faded art prints over a bureau heaped with clothes. A broken lamp in the corner. A rectangle of light marking the bathroom door.

Next morning I woke up alone. I could hear Marie's motorcycle. I could hear voices talking below, a drone, tones only, no words. My husband came up to me with coffee, and I bargained with him for our last thousand dollars on the grounds that I had bought his Ph.D. Rashak wanted to throw the kids into the deal. "If you get the money," he argued, "you get the kids. I can't raise them on nothing." Rashak's fortune.

Meanwhile, downstairs Ramji was announcing that Jennifer and Hanna had lice. He could see tiny white eggs nestled in the hair that lined the base of their skulls. Ingrid yelled up at us in case we hadn't heard. It riled Lewis. He shouted, blaming me, dragging me down to look at the kids, charging me with gross child neglect. Marie came behind him trying to calm his panic, but he raged on. Sanitary conditions in the house, he shouted, were such that his guts were ravaged by parasites. All my fault.

He came from the kitchen and hurled a carton of milk at me. "Why is this stinking sour milk always put back in the refrigerator? I have to throw out most of my coffee." Jenny was standing in the door screaming. Marie had moved into the living room, crying, staring out the window. Ramji beat a hasty retreat to the garden for a quick meditation. And Ingrid, a head taller and a foot wider, advanced on Rashak. She hefted the little prick off the floor and slapped his face. I watched it all as though it had nothing to do with me. They were like cartoon characters: Lewis off the ground, trying to smash the big Viking, but she just grabbed his wrist.

"You and that fakir can get the hell out of here," he

yelled. "Go to a fucking hotel. Go to hell. Just get out of here." Ramji was like an ivory carving placed in the garden, his head bowed, his hands folded.

Three days later Marie left for Paris. I could only attribute it to second thoughts about Lewis. Sooner or later everyone has second thoughts about Lewis. But he went into agony when she left. He began questioning me constantly about Mwema, insisting that the affair was shameful, a laughing stock. Mwema was married: he left his wife in some foul village rotting away with their kids while he fucked white women in town. "Where do you go?" he harped. He continued to want details, which I couldn't give. He badgered me, followed me around with threats. Finally, when he couldn't stand it anymore (he said) he took half our money and bought himself a round-trip ticket to France.

"I have to get away from you and that coon," he said. "You're driving me insane with your behavior."

"You bastard,"—I was furious—"it was supposed to be my money."

And his incredible answer: "I divided it. In any divorce, the property gets divided in half."

"Give me half the Ph.D. then." I felt like someone who had just lost a bet, who didn't know she had been gambling.

I could easily have taken the rest of the money, or even used my return ticket to go with him and then home with the kids, but it never crossed my mind. I must have wanted to stay even though I felt deserted when he left. The last part of being held up is watching your assailant get away, how you want to shout, "COME BACK!" with your arm raised, your mouth opened, stunned to your bones. My mirror told me he'd left me shabbier than ever, threadbare, like a garment that's been washed for the last time.

Jenny begged me, "Mommy, please, get up,"

because she sensed I'd been in bed too long. And I knew I had, too. She was pulling my arm, weeping.

I remembered how Ingrid kept saying, "Look to yourself, Marlene. You look too much to Lewis." When I did look to myself, I saw there had to be some point to my coming to Africa, because it hadn't saved my marriage. More than just the memory I would have of John Mwema, I wanted to take something back, and it had to be something real that I could touch—an object—the way that people travel halfway around the world to; places like Iran so they can bring back carpets, or to China for vases. And vases made me think of pots, and pots made me think of my pots, and maybe it was a silly thing, but I wanted to succeed in what I had tried to do when we first got here, to make something from the clay I dug so happily in the riverbed. A pot, like the beautiful pots that African women made, from start to finish, fired in my own kiln. And, for once, it didn't defeat me to look at the dust in the crisis of my living room, or the dried lumps of clay, or the kiln out there on the hillside, the shambles.

I wasn't sure when Lewis would come back from Paris, so I moved fast. I took the rest of the money. I bought real fire bricks. I built a real kiln. I watered and softened and worked my clay, kneading it, resting it, the cycles of getting it ready. I saw myself, a figure rounded to a task, shoulders and arms, as determined as earth. Mwema helped me. He helped me build the kiln and clean my house, repair the broken screens and furniture. The Danish couple knew about a small potter's wheel for sale that once had belonged to their ambassador's wife. I bought it and moved it to my living room, a real studio now, facing the window, the hill that fell away to dark ferns in the riverbed where lilies that looked like candy grew.

Lewis stayed in Paris a month.

"Everything changed," he told me when he came back. He didn't want to talk about it. It must have flopped with Marie and it was hard on him. He was thinner than ever and his skin seemed shriveled. There were lines near his eyes and mouth that hadn't been there before. It amazed me that I felt sorry for him, even as I saw him try to manipulate—oh, he was so pleased to see I finally had my shit together, was working at last—trying to make it seem that he was part of it, but I wasn't the old Marlene anymore and he shouldn't have bothered.

"None of it matters much, Lewis," I told him. Perhaps I sounded dreamy. I think he thought I meant to forgive him and in ways I could do that, looking down, looking all around as he came close, because I was so much larger than he was, his hand on my neck, his lips, though he agreed, yes, he could wait, would wait until I was ready again, until the whole terrible year had been forgotten.

You learn to be fatalistic in the tropics. Or maybe it's just that you learn to be fatalistic when you're far away because there's nothing you control, not even the language. A language you don't understand reminds you how vulnerable you are. I knew that when Lewis's contract was up, the university wouldn't renew it and our visas would expire and then we would have to leave. That was a certain destiny. Even now, I can't say what it meant to Mwema and me to live that way, the feeling of a marked-out time. I think of tropical flowers with petals that burn and bleed, and I think of breaking things. But this isn't meant to be about him, or about how we managed to say good-bye.

The day we left, the Danish couple received a shipment of cheese from home and we sat with them and several other expatriates to share it. Paper-thin slices and aromatic chunks circulated. We sipped at the wine. No one in the room had even looked at a piece of cheese in months, but a decorum of self-restraint operated at the table. What held us back, mouths watering, when all we wanted to do was grab?

Lewis was too nervous to eat anything. He stood aside going through the standard motions of an air traveler, studying his ticket, his passport, his health card, fearing they might contain some hitch he hadn't seen, a detail that would abort the journey. Our winter coats were draped on a chair, portents, crumbled and faded as curtains in an old derelict theater, closing on some final scene. The room smelled of their storage— mildew and mothballs.

"Will there be snow?" Hanna asked.

"Snow snow snow!" Jenny was singing.

"Is it winter there now?" one of the Danes asked. They all smiled. "So easy to forget," he said.

My suitcase was nearest to the door and next to it was the pot I had chosen from the ones I made to carry back, so big it was ridiculous and I'd have to keep it on my lap like a baby. I still have it, a classic African beer pot, wide bellied, with a small mouth and a curving rim. Even now, when I see my pots on display in shows and shops, pressed into wild shapes from dreams and memories, when I see how much my work has changed, I like that simple, strong vessel the best and often wonder how I made it. The walls are too thin to hold the curve or to have survived the fire, and the symmetry is perfect despite the poor clay I used.

We flew home through two days and a night, Lewis and I, talking and talking because I knew we couldn't stay together and he didn't. The children played and slept. And each time the plane landed in West Africa, looking out on tarmac and the fringe of palms, lights that lifted jungles from the dark, the kids asked, "Are we out of Africa yet?"

And each time, I told them, no.

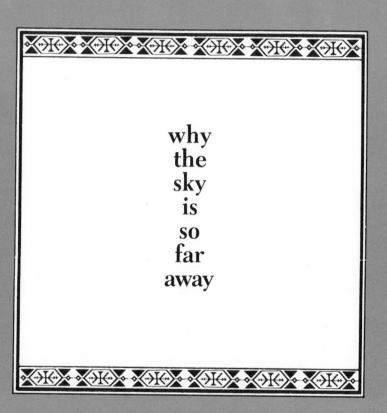

why
the
sky
is
so
far
away

Steve Williams railed against the sky. He tried to charge it. Over the chain-link, the darkened runway, into the waiting craft, the cockpit of an empty plane. But the police got him, pulled him out screaming and fighting. Thin, strong, black cops in shorts, carrying clubs. They shot him with drugs at the station. Peace Corps: they knew it. He spoke Amharic like a native, had been in Ethiopia for four years. He held back his name. Then Denver Cox came, talked them into a sort of bail, and sent him to Jordan's house, to his friends and more drugs.

In the morning things were not that much better. Tony Albanuso, grinning through his beard, was offering two whores. The girls, all demure, were twittering behind him. But Williams couldn't make it; he felt as though he were still pulling away from the malaria, as though his eyeballs, still bilious from his jaundice, were spiraling patterns. He looks at Albanuso, psychedelic Albanuso, fourteen grins going around.

"But I wasn't high. Not then . . ." His voice cracks, a broken laugh. "I sort of thought I could . . ." Growing embarrassed, he stares at his greasy Jockey shorts, the elastic popping out like misplaced hairs. "We've eaten too much sky," he tells Albanuso again. "It's retreating in fury. Rains will stop and the sun will put away." He sounds hollow, as if his long sicknesses have worn him away, like a syphilis victim disintegrating from within, spinal column pulverizing to dust.

The weather in Addis is hot. Then every night a chill comes on and the transients at Jordan's house roll out sleeping bags and pile over each other while Claude Applehouse grumbles in the background. Applehouse thinks that Jordan has left him in charge, so he supervises. It's futile. Already some of the potted plants have died. They barbecued three of Jordan's rabbits and used up his typewriter ribbon and all his airmail envelopes. No one cleans the place. Rat turds the size of bullets are showing up everywhere. Worse, a water shortage has eliminated the possibility of flushing the toilet and the bathroom blazes op-art scatological signs about what to do and not do in there. As the sun pulls around the corner of the house and blasts in a window over the desert of dead plants, Albanuso and the two whores appear from Williams's room. The girls flow behind in their white dresses like brown saints. They giggle and fade out the door. It pisses Applehouse off.

"Albanuso," Applehouse says in a loud whisper, pushing the girls out of the way, "what am I supposed to do with *him?*" They have this idea that Albanuso can handle Williams. That Albanuso knows the story. Albanuso, after all, is Williams's buddy. It was Albanuso who had tried to explain to Cox what had happened at the airport, how Williams had gone back out into the field with him and Stringfellow (maybe too soon) when he was still sick, still had a fever, still had the clap, still had jaundice; how Williams thought if he started working again he might get better, how things in Ethiopia these days were so bad, so bad, how your body and your mind . . . He tried to explain it. And Cox nodded. But anyone could see Cox didn't know what was happening at all.

Williams was still sick, but he had gone out with Albanuso, his main man, and Stringfellow, their third, because he wanted to get well again and work hard again. The three of them had their reputations to uphold—the record number of vaccinations in one day. Three thousand. Their own private campaign to eradicate smallpox from the world. Those three thousand had flocked out of their houses, streaming down on Williams, Albanuso, and Stringfellow like a wave on a swollen muddy river, brown and churning and yelling for medicine. Poor Stringfellow quaked, a hypochondriac of the worst sort; he started vaccinating himself every other week.

"Sometimes it takes!" he wails. "It means I coulda got it!"

Williams had grown tired of the scene at Jordan's. He had always thought of the place as home base but suddenly he found he was older than the others. He had been around longer, had done more and knew more than all of them put together. Things were wearing away somehow and he was beginning to feel shabby, like the rubble at the house, the transients, the unflushed can, the rat turds everywhere. He had once been happy to rush into town tossing off stories that had everyone Williams-worshipping, but lately he had borne down on everyone with a ridicule that was tearing his chances for friendship and leaving him stranded. Sometimes he thought he was waiting for his time here to finish, but sometimes he thought that this time was all he ever would have and he was wasting it. It was like something catching up to him, cluttering around him so he couldn't move.

When Albanuso showed up to take him away, he felt relieved. He would join Albanuso and Stringfellow again. It looked like a chance to mend. Albanuso had tales of epidemics in the north. A drought of three years, he said, had the people wandering around in search of food, carrying the disease with them like a currency of damnation. Williams agreed to go. Jaundice, clap, malaria, or no. Somehow the work was everything. He could act like someone driven. Once he walked alone into a remote village. His Ethiopian assistants had refused to go. They claimed the tribesmen collected testicles. Even white ones. Williams went in anyway, carrying his vaccine and going through the torture of being polite to the chief. He drank horrible curdled milk, ate raw meat, and took salt and rancid butter in his coffee, just to get permission to inoculate. "Still have my balls!" he boasted on his return, hand cupped between his legs.

They greeted him in Addis like Agamemnon on his returns. There were times when it felt good to think of himself as he thought they thought of him, but he knew that most of them didn't really like him. "Who can stand that prick Williams?" he overheard Applehouse say. It all made him feel he was getting as severed from the world he had been building for himself here as he was from the world he had left four years ago. He felt more and more drawn to something he wasn't sure of, something he only hoped to find. He could see that he had been speeding through, taking what he wanted, but he was moving—it was a paradox—slowly, with a sense that everything he left behind unused would drag him down. He felt at times, despite his conviction of being better and smarter than everyone else, that he was an affront. But to what? Nature? Mankind? He got along by doing everything in excess. No matter what his condition. Hadn't he let this girl, Caitlin Wonder, a volunteer who often crashed at Jordan's, jerk him off (and he, her) with all the others in sleeping bags around him and he sizzling and freezing and coming at the same time? (He hadn't screwed her because he was feeling honest and he still had the clap.)

So even though he was still sick, he agreed to go up north with Albanuso and Stringfellow. He wanted to get back to something that made sense—stopping a disease. What made more sense? Herr Doktor Banhoffer, the director of their program, a frantic Kraut who worked for the U.N., planned the route for them.

"Something is happening up there," said the good Bavarian, splotchy white and city fat, his remaining russet hairs standing up in perpetual surprise, his head indented as if a meteor had landed on him, blasted his brain, and popped his eyes out in front.

"I'll tell you what is happening hup dere," Albanuso mimicked the Herr Doktor outside his office. "There's a famine up there and the good baron knows it. They're coming out of the anthills with every disease known to mankind, the apocalypse, the first rider, riding a death horse black as Mother Africa's arse-hole." He played every syllable, a reminder of the old days when he read poetry in the coffee houses of Boston. They could feel Stringfellow shrinking behind them.

"When did you get your last typhoid shot?" Stringfellow mumbled. He had already vaccinated himself twice but didn't get a take. "I'm either immune," he said, looking at his pathetic arm full of scratches, "or the vaccine is no good. Albanuso, is it possible to get a bad batch?"

Albanuso rolled his eyes in an attitude of prayer. He had been studying Islam lately and was muttering something about Allah in Arabic. They put up with Stringfellow because he would work like hell. He was one of the few.

"Rumors have it," Albanuso went on, "that the women are laying their babies in the road. You can't be sure if they're trying to get you to stop so they can beg food, or if they want you to run over them."

They blasted out of town over the mountains in a Land Rover stuffed with grass. From the top they looked into a great gash, a shocking slate V in the earth where baboons sat on ledges, manes as large as lions', their shrill cries amplified in the cone. They pressed through a string of grim towns, vaccinating steadily in what looked

like refugee camps along the road. People had been filtering out, looking for food. Thousands. On the edge of
starvation.

"How can there be so many of them?" Stringfellow
moaned. The people descended like furies on the few
cars that passed. "Oh, look," Stringfellow cried, "their
eyes, their eyes are infected. There's pus. What is it?"

Williams wondered if he could take it this time. He
was only half available during the days and then, at night,
he had a frantic need to dig up some whore because he
wanted her sex as much as he wanted to talk about it in
the morning, betraying the girl with his comments about
her body, about whether she had a clitoridectomy, about
her tits. Each morning he woke feeling more detached
from his work and from the world. Nothing seemed to
have a context. It was as if Nature were pulling back with
a loud voice saying, *"You've done enough. Everything in
between is gone, and when it does rain, all the rest is going
to wash away."*

"I hate to say it," he mumbled to Stringfellow, "but
it would be better if they all died." They stood in front of
a desperate crowd, a gang, brown and heaped like trash.
The thought alone was breaking him, a distance he
didn't think he could ever go. He resented these people
for the ruined bits they had become, and he resented
the earth for ceasing to offer, and he resented himself
for still caring.

They turn east then, down the escarpment toward
the Red Sea. They pass ancient salt mines, vast stretches
of evaporated seas. Dead cattle litter the road, bodies
bent into eerie sculptures. Vultures are stuffed and bask
in the trees. Dogs and hyenas run fat. Stringfellow turns
alternately green and purple as they pass the Danakil
men, armed to the teeth, hair wild and uncut, looking
mean as hell. Albanuso tells him there aren't any bullets
in their guns, but Stringfellow brings up the spears they

balance across their shoulders, the big knives at their waists, and the small ones stuck to their afros. His talking can go on for hours.

"Not in this heat, Stringfellow," says Williams. "I can't deal with it." It must be one hundred twenty degrees. Albanuso claims there is no way they will get these nomads to agree to inoculation.

"Let's go back then," says Stringfellow. "They're all going to die."

Some of the camels are dying and the Danakil are out on the road—two very bad signs because camels don't die easily and these tribesmen prefer to wander secretly in their desert and never come out to look around. But they're out now and looking hungry.

"Why isn't it in all the papers?" Williams asks.

"They have chosen to—er, overlook it, let's say," says Albanuso.

"Overlook it? They *know*?" Stringfellow, sterilizing his needles in the cookfire.

"I did not say they knew," says Albanuso. "They can't afford to know."

"But it hasn't rained for three years, man. They have to know," says Williams.

"They *suspect*. Can't you hear it now?" Albanuso rattles, throwing his voice down a couple notches to patronizing-important. "We suspect, gentlemen, that there may just be a drought. Of course we cannot verify this. It may start raining any day now. Meteorologically speaking, it's all hypothetical. Like, you don't see anybody around here checking it out."

"Except us."

"Make no mistake. We are doing *something else*," Albanuso's outrage has worn down and now he figures the best thing is to find work and do it hard. Like sticking thousands of people with smallpox vaccine so they can starve to death within a year. To some it would make no sense: to Albanuso it makes all kinds of sense.

"You piss me off," Williams tells him. Going around with Albanuso for four years had Williams convinced that he had changed. Now he feels he's still stuck in the patterns worked out for him years ago and someplace else: the gluttony to excel at any cost, to reach the high standards he set for himself and the world. He wanted to be like Albanuso instead.

When he first met Tony Albanuso he had seen something that canceled the tight life he'd left behind—the cramped New Jersey suburb, the isolation and protection of Dartmouth College, the dean's list, the plans for law school. His mother had been disappointed when he announced that he was joining the Peace Corps. She walked away in icy fury when he came home two years later and told them that he had signed on for another two years. His father had barked at him like a dog. What if they ever met his friend Albanuso, the son of Lebanese immigrants, a "poet" with a mouthful of weird images and a stick of hash in his lips? Albanuso was the first person Williams met who never lied. If you didn't lie, Albanuso said, there were no big prices to pay, except that holding on to truth was sometimes painful: you had to put it where no one could get it.

Still, despite everything, Williams remained the kid he had tried to bump off, the achiever, the "prick," the son of his parents and his whole town. What he had been sloughing off, it seemed, was his ability to love. Not in general terms—he was aware how intensely he felt for these tired humans he saw every day—but in specific terms, with the people he should have been close to. With his parents, whom he had written off. Even with Albanuso and Stringfellow, his best friends. He had failed for the most part with girls, sometimes physically, always emotionally. There had never been *one* girl. He was good looking, and he used it until—with the light out, when he could no longer be seen—everything retreated and his spirit as well as his penis went limp. He was afraid of the lies, the ones he told and the ones others told him.

With Albanuso, for the first time in his life, he thought he could live in a low-cost way. He built the image, the reflection he caught of boisterousness in Albanuso that had been dormant all his life. But there were times like this when Albanuso infuriated him.

"I've got the truth stuffed up my ass, see, where no one can get it. . . ." Albanuso, the anal erotic, ridiculous. Well, he could keep it dirtied like that if that's what he really wanted. Williams doubted. Now they were facing a test. Williams could feel the rift between them.

"You expect too much, Steve boy," Albanuso says in this now-I'm-going-to-tell-you-something-you-knew voice. "Anyone can see, especially down here, that there is nothing left." How then, Williams wonders, can Albanuso go on laughing?

At daybreak they drive by compass over trackless black lava fields, the haunted remains of some Jurassic upheaval as bare as a dead planet. They pick up a lone man along the way who says he knows an encampment where there is smallpox and a disease of the bowels.

"If he doesn't stink, we'll take him," Albanuso whispers over his shoulder after greeting the old man, surprised to find he speaks Arabic. "He's a Hadji," Albanuso says, indicating to Stringfellow to make room in the back.

"I guess we take him even if he does stink," Stringfellow bitches.

"But he doesn't," says Williams as the old man passes behind him.

"The Hadji comes from West Africa," Albanuso translates, "never made it back from Mecca. He's been wandering around for years. There's no telling how much he knows."

The old man offers around a pouch of *chat*, the local narcotic leaf, organic speed. They stop the Land Rover and, in its shadow, chew the bitter leaves. It's like freon chilling their veins. Williams, feeling his head open up, stares into the obsidian eyes of the Hadji. He can sense there are rules that this old man knows; sees him like a bolt of air sheared stark with no junk hanging off him. It's like staring at a second chance, if he can only grab it somehow, to end the rift in his mind between what he feels and sees and what he might have to do with it later.

As the night freezes up into an empty sky, they can see the lights of the encampment. Stringfellow is already complaining about the stench of the camels. He is panic-stricken that someone might make him drink that awful mixture of blood and milk.

Albanuso says, "Just hold your breath and strain it through your teeth, the clots, see, like this . . ." Poor Stringfellow looks so bad. Just two short years ago he was one hundred pounds heavier, now his clothes hang on him like the banners of a defeated army. And Williams is laughing at it all, because he thinks he has seen something that will finally release him and not just dazzle him as Albanuso has done.

At the encampment the next day they vaccinate like hell. The old man rounds up customers, showing his own scar, gold teeth flashing, knife clicking against his hard bones. At the end of it, when Albanuso is at his highest (like a drunk, crowds intoxicate him), they are taken to a tent set aside, and because they are doctors and have medicine, they are shown the dying people. The smell is so bad that it ceases to matter. They have never seen cholera before. Never smelled it. But there it is. They stare and apologize and explain that they are not really doctors and there is nothing they can do.

"We have to do something!" wails Stringfellow, half mad, half crying.

"We can wash our hands. That's all. For Christ's sake," answers Albanuso at his absolute worst. At his *worst*, thinks Williams, torn between what he feels he

should do—the truth he wants to hold up to the world—
and his own helplessness against the world's great
callousness and corruption. What had happened to that
clear, cold vision of the day before, that chance he saw as
blue, as sharp as the sky? It was gone.

Stringfellow is sterilizing everything, trying to boil
his clothes, and urging Albanuso to abandon the old man.

"Don't be ridiculous, that old man isn't really
human, he doesn't get diseases," says Albanuso, pouring
some coffee.

The moon is wild over them, silver in an empty sky.
The old man talks to Albanuso, his Arabic is enormous, a
spoken calligraphy. The sound alone draws pictures.
Albanuso translates:

> Delicious, the sky tempted men, who hacked
> off slabs of it that they never finished. They left
> pieces in rubbish heaps where it remained dark and
> unlighted by the sun. They excreted it undigested
> in great mounds. The cast-off pieces irritated the
> sky. It sent down warnings of thunder and lightning.
> It held off its rains or it poured down in floods. It
> will finally retreat in anger. From this place it has
> been retreating for many years. Men here will
> starve and sicken. Far away, in other places, they
> climb to it in airplanes. They are gorged with it and
> the rot is all around them. They are bloated and
> they have a stinking breath.

The story slaps Williams like a great joke through
the haze of the grass he's smoking. He can hear himself
laughing. He says, "We're shitting out the sky!"

Albanuso says, "But, hey, we're not so full of shit as
the fuckers chopping off the Big Pieces."

Next day they decide to head quickly for the Red
Sea. They drop the old man at the next encampment.

People along the road are so desperate they don't object to vaccinations.

"I can't stand any more!" says Stringfellow, yawning, thinner than ever, with dark circles under his eyes and gums as pale as his teeth. Drying out, Williams thinks. Like I am. Turning to dust. Pissing and pissing until there is nothing left, his water spreading fragile sheets on the canvas floor—sparkling salt mines. He licks the salt, bent on his knees. Albanuso catches him. Albanuso stares. Not saying a word.

"I don't feel too good," Williams tells him by way of an explanation. What could it explain?

Albanuso is afraid, but all he can say is, "Hey, man, let's go down to the sea again. Ball those good women on the coast."

"I don't need it," Williams says. "I want to go back to Cox and Banhoffer to tell them."

"They won't do anything! You're wasting your fucking time," Albanuso says. "You'll have to go back without me. I'm not that dumb."

"Hey, please take me back," he pleads.

So they speed back to Addis in a horrible dust storm. They almost hit an aardvark. Williams is ranting. The aardvark is a sign: only strange creatures could survive, beasts that ate insects.

When they reach town, Williams forces them to take him immediately to Denver Cox. Cox is nervous, bored by their arrogance. He has no stand.

Back in the Land Rover, Williams stares out the windshield. "Take me to Jordan's," he says. He doesn't have the energy to find a hotel and he doesn't want to be alone. He wants things to be the way they were, but as he walks through the door, he knows he doesn't like the company at Jordan's anymore. They are all stoned. He walks past them to one of the back bedrooms.

Over the next few days, Williams calls Denver Cox again and again. Cox keeps telling him to wait until tomorrow. They won't let him quit. It's getting so that Williams can't even say to himself what he wanted to tell them. He has to clear out. He is becoming claustrophobic and impotent. So he runs quietly to the airport, climbs the fence, and enters the plane.

"Denver, of course, said something absurd," Albanuso reports. "He thinks everything is going to be okay. We should cool it, he says."

"Why won't he come out of his room?" Caitlin Wonder whines. "Should I go in there?"

"He'll come out," Albanuso assures her.

And in two days he does. Naked. His room is foul. He's been urinating on the floor.

"I want to tell the Congress," he announces, "about the sky." He mumbles a stream of loud sounds, something about diseases. Applehouse is vibrating at the desk. Someone has got "Bye-Bye Miss American Pie" blaring on the record player so no one can hear Williams speak. They see only his amber skin, his gaunt face, his beard. Albanuso rushes to him, takes his arm, covers him with a blanket. Albanuso feels like he will float away. He's like a deflated balloon starting to fill with air. He feels it puff under his eyes, forming pockets like ripples around his neck. From under Albanuso's arm, he scans the room, then searches his dark friend's eyes. Faces surge at him, distorted in the mirror of Albanuso's black pupils. He feels as though he has eaten something huge and tasteless. He's stuffed but not satisfied. He has the urge to gag, to throw it up, but he holds the truth like Albanuso holds his truth, filled with it, floating high and away from earth with it. He wants to vomit or drop it like a bird that has scavenged a dump. His scream slashes the sky; his yell falls on the rubble.

summer
opportunity

Mr. and Mrs. Warren P. Stegler request the pleasure of the company of *Ms. Gwendolyn Johnson* at a reception on *Tuesday July 2* from 7:00–9:00 P.M.

182 Embassy Crescent

RSVP (regrets only)   Tel. 01627

and written below:

"To welcome Ms. Gwendolyn Johnson
to Lagos, Summer IDI program."

Gwendolyn leans back, fingers the invite like a playing card, and takes a drag on her Benson & Hedges (airplane stash: duty free). She tries it on, "Beens'n 'n Hey-ges! Whoooooo? I say, Ben-Son and Hedge-Es." She tries IDI, "Ah-dee-ah," laughs around a little, and says, "I-D-I spells In-ter-na-tion-al Deee-vel-op-ment In-tern. Me." Summer program means minority program. Minority summer opportunity. An opportunity for a minority for a summer.

"Gwind'lin!" her mother had shouted when she heard about the trip six months ago, "You ain't goin' to *no Africa.*"

Gwendolyn's mother never got used to minority opportunity. Way back in the fourth grade in Mississippi, sometime in the middle sixties, Gwendolyn had been selected to integrate the white school.

"Oh, yeah, well they's 'on haf ta come git you!" her mother hollered; and when the white social worker showed up to drag the girl off to school, Ida Johnson (five foot ten and two hundred pounds) picked up the skinny, pale lady and heaved her out of the front yard—never opened the gate.

But they finally got Gwendolyn for the ninth grade and kept her right through high school. She had no friends save that skin-and-bones Ralphy Wilkins, the other minority with an opportunity. Those two looked like Jack Sprat and his wife. Gwendolyn was already beginning to look like her mother. But she did very well in school and graduated in the top fifteen percent of her class. She was selected for an IBM minority training program. It meant she would have to go to New York. The night before she was to leave, Mrs. Johnson set fire to her suitcase while the girl wailed in her room and her brothers and sisters roared with laughter.

She had to say home. Miserable. Fat Gwendolyn. In her room, she ate potato chips, drank Cokes, cried herself silly, and read novels. Her mother wanted her to forget IBM and get a job in town waiting tables or running the cash register at the local grocery store. "You work for black folks or you be sorry," she said. Gwendolyn refused. She was too ashamed to be seen around town. She tried to explain to her mother that she had been given opportunities. Now she was a failure. And no fault of her own.

"I coulda gone places," she told her brother Melchior. "Don't you let Mamma tromp you down." Melchior also went to the white high school and was already at the top of his class. Melchior told Gwendolyn not to worry; he had an idea that would take her places. From the library at school, he got college catalogues for his sister. Black colleges. Exclusively for black kids.

Melchior's idea was that Mamma would agree to that. And so it was. Gwendolyn: on a big scholarship to Howard.

"Satan's own Washington!" her mother moaned.

"Chocolate city, they calls it," Uncle Charlie said. And they pressed the frightened Ida Johnson into agreeing.

Gwendolyn threw herself right into things at Howard. Before she had been there a month, this Melchior sent her a little button said, BLACK IS BEAUTIFUL. And it was. Howard girls with their afros and tinted shades, their slender butts and their bouncy braless tits. Howard cats, tall, flat-bellied, shiny big afros, dashikis, sandals, and pants tight on their slick sides.

Gwendolyn did not date. She was too fat. But the kids liked Gwen. She always had the joke. At Howard she got herself a style. She wore tent dresses in bright African prints, cut her hair into a huge, high afro, and covered herself with lots of cheap bangles and necklaces. She bought lots of big fringed shawls.

Now, one day, over on 11th Street, this Gwendolyn is walking, humming and swaying her lots of flesh side to side. She just made honor grades again and she's on the way to something special. She's just a leeetle high—a postprandial pipe with Walter Jackson and Sally B. A Washington spring, and black folks are out and turning on. In the window of this little hole-in-the-wall, factory-to-you-prices, no-name shoe store, Gwendolyn sees the sandals of every woman's dreams. No white cat of a shoe man ever made those steppers.

"These shoes," the man inside tells her, "are custom designed. One fine lady over Alexandria had them made special. But like it go," he says, "she hit bad luck. Never come git 'em. Now, young lady, you ain' never gonna see a-nuvver pair of shoes like these!"

Gwen smiles, puts them on, and struts her stuff, just a little top heavy on these four-inch platforms.

"On'y the fines' leather," the man tells her—thin

leather straps in twelve dark, wild colors woven into dazzling baskets out of which peeks the shocking pink of Gwendolyn's toenails. "Ever' place you goes," the man says, "people gon' look at you an' say, *Lookit 'em shoes!*"

And they did. In Mississippi, when Gwen went home for spring vacation, people went pale and speechless in the wake of those shoes. And her mother, accusing Gwendolyn of having become a whore, threatened to destroy the sandals.

"You a fine howdy-do!" her mother told her, tossing the shoes at her.

Gwendolyn told Uncle Charlie first. An intercessor. "The government has picked me to go on a program to Africa. 'Count I got good grades and things. They gonna pay me all kind a money jes' to write a paper. I get a trip, my credits at school, and a chance for a job when I get out. Tell Mamma I'll buy her a new stove and icebox the day I get home. It's only for three month," she said. "You tell Mamma."

"AFRICA!" she heard her mother roar in the other room, and then the phrases coming in an excited garble: ". . . wil' animals . . . heyd huntahs . . . mumbo jumbo . . . too many niggers . . ." Gwendolyn smiled at Melchior, the two of them down on the floor with an atlas, looking for Nigeria.

Gwendolyn packed up to get out of there in a hurry in case Mrs. Johnson had a change of mind. As it was, her mother vacillated, threatening to drown herself or take the gas pipe or do both to Gwendolyn. She was frightened, she allowed in one of her quieter moments, that Gwendolyn might not come home. Not because her daughter might get hurt—what could be worse than Satan's own Washington?—but because her daughter might just like it there.

"When you walk down the street," she mused, "an' someone there in a car or standing behin' a tree, or comin' out 'roun' a corner . . . when a man got his back to you and that man turn 'roun', his face gonna be a black face."

"Yeah, an' all the cops be black," said Uncle Charlie.

"All the doctors, the nurses, the judges, the pilots," said Melchior.

"All the teachers," said Sukie.

"An' telephone operators," said Phyllis.

"Car sellers and car buyers," said Roger.

"Car fixers and car builders," said Benjamin.

Gwendolyn and her brothers and sisters danced around the table. They made a party with Cokes and chocolate cakes and a banner saying, BON VOYAGE, GWEN BABY.

When Gwendolyn arrived in Lagos, Nigeria, a Mrs. Stegler was at the airport to welcome her and drive her to a small flat. She was a slender blond woman and she smiled and chatted about what life was like in this hectic town. Perhaps Gwendolyn was tired, she suggested, perhaps Gwendolyn would like a day or two to rest. "Jet lag," she called it, a phrase that made Gwendolyn feel like she had just *arrived*, honey, not *lagged*. Gwendolyn Johnson in the jet set. Gwendolyn thanked the lady, plopped down on a couch, and expected to sleep, but she was wound up, like the highest high, she was tuning in on all channels, running on all cylinders.

She opened up her big, new, red suitcase, pulled out her big blue jeans, her bright green, sleeveless turtleneck jersey and her multicolored four-inch platform sandals. Ready for battle on the town. She grabbed a bus in what she reckoned was the right direction, hit what looked like the downtown, and wound up in a place called Dixie Fried Chicken, with a menu right out of Colonel Sanders and a picture of some black dude in a Colonel Sanders outfit smiling out of a kinky beard and saying, "Real U.S. fried chicken. Try our crinkle-fry chips

and fish burgers." Right there she met her first man, a
skinny kid about half her size. He made the proposition
and she didn't hesitate. She grabbed the opportunity and
took him back to the flat and stayed there with him until
the next day.

And then, two nights later, there was the Hausa
trader, a tall wiry man, very black but with the features
of a white man. He wore a long shirtlike thing and an
embroidered skull cap. He chewed on kola nut and
betel and his fine mouth was tinted deep red. He
smelled of leather and came to her door selling statues
and hassocks. She had just had a bath and had tied herself in a robe, pulling the sash tight around her waist.
His eyes froze on her breasts when she leaned forward
to look at his wares. She made the Hausa shower first
and then, still wet, he twisted his long ebony body
around her like a snake, his breath perfumed with betel
nut. She bought a carving from him, a ripe woman holding out huge breasts over a big belly and carefully
etched below, the fine details of her sex. "Like this dude
had statues that looked like *me*," she wrote in an X-rated
letter to Sally B. at Howard.

When Ellie Stegler called Gwendolyn to say, "We
would like to have a welcoming get-together for you,
Gwen," Gwendolyn wanted to say, "Missus, I already
been welcomed!"

Instead, she said, "Oh, thank you, Mrs. Stegler, I'd
really like that." Summer opportunity. The invitation
went in her scrapbook along with the plane ticket vouch-
ers and the chit from the Dixie Fried Chicken. "Shittin'
in the tall corn, as we say in Mississippi," she muttered,
thinking, An' I'm gonna razzle dazzle them with my coon
shoes, four big inches up, soaring over the host and hostess sky high.

The reception, your typical honky do with the
chamber music muted in the background and scrawny

white ladies on diets dwarfed in big African caftans, was a good time after all. Practically all the Nigerian guys, guys who worked in the office, guys who worked in the ministries alongside American technicians, guys who were teachers at American-sponsored colleges, guys who studied in the States, all these guys clustered around Gwendolyn. She was American, rich (so they thought), in transit, so clearly loose, and she was *magnificent.* Before the night was over, she had four dates for the next night. She somehow intended to keep them all.

She ended up going out with the first guy that showed. His name was Adedeji. He took her to dinner. He told her about the couple of years he spent in the States at Yale University, freezing his ass off and pumping gas to get pocket money. He told her about his village in Western State, about his family, his father who had seven wives.

"But I'll only have one wife," he told her. He took her to his small flat. He took her to his bed. He told her she was beautiful and sweet. He said it in Yoruba. *O dun. O wu mi.* A language that rose and fell like a song.

She laughed, "Hey, you know, back home, I'm just fat Gwendolyn. I tell jokes."

"Here you are a goddess," only he wasn't joking. He caressed her rich flesh, the mound of her belly. He tasted the thick folds of her neck.

Gwendolyn breaks all her other dates forever. When the Hausa comes, she tells him she doesn't want any tee-hee. When the skinny kid from the Dixie Fried shows up, she doesn't invite him in. She spends all her time with Adedeji. She should be writing her paper, doing her research. Grabbing the opportunity. But she doesn't even go into the office.

Mrs. Stegler checks in: "Is everything okay, Gwen? Is there any kind of problem? I don't want to pry, but if I can help . . ." She starts saying things that sound like they're supposed to make Gwendolyn feel responsible, possibly grateful, as though she were standing there for her whole race and her whole sex. She's using tired old phrases like ". . . times of change . . . black women in demand in the job market of the future . . . a real chance . . . a golden opportunity."

Gwendolyn interrupts, "You don't mind me asking this do you, but, like, what are you, personally, doing about all these movements—all this stuff you're laying on me?"

Ellie Stegler looks kind of embarrassed. "I don't know what I'm doing. I'm sorry. I wish I was your age. I wish I had your chance."

"Okay, okay, I'll get the work done," Gwen tells her, with absolutely no intention of doing a thing.

Adedeji invites her to come to his village for a few days. She agrees, excited. She goes with him dressed in Yoruba duds, a wrapper and a *gele*, the wild turban of Western Nigeria, big as a dream flower opening on the wide African morning. On her platform sandals she is nearly as tall as he is. He gives her a golden bangle that she knows he can't afford. He takes her picture with his instant camera, twice, giving one print to her and keeping the other for himself. And there she is, beaming in Kodacolor, rainbow Gwen, looking for all the world like an authentic, indigenous, Yoruba native.

On the bus, she loosens the wrapper. Air rushes into the folds of the cloth over her hot, moist skin. Adedeji looks cool, used to the heat. People talk in Yoruba to her and she laughs, telling them that she is American. Maybe she is Yoruba, she tells Adedeji. They buy boxes of yogurt and spicy cakes made of mashed beans, eggs, sardines, and hot pepper, steamed in green leaves.

"Just like my Mamma said," she tells Adedeji. "I see a little kid behind a bush, a woman bent over a child, a guy resting on his belly in the shade: I see that person there ahead of me standing in the dark shadow of a porch

and I don't have to worry or even go close up to see his
face. I know he's black. You understand what that
means?" Did she really believe it though? Did her
mother really believe it? That there was safety in color?
That no one here would hurt her? She drank the light as it
washed over Adedeji's perfect face, modeled on soft
curves, his almond eyes set high on his cheekbones,
strangely Oriental eyes, and his skin, not brown like hers
but dark, jet black. She wondered if her mother had been
right, if she might not just stay here with this man. Why
was he taking her to his home? Was it a proposal?

His father's compound—enclosed in high terra-
cotta walls, clouded in red dust, a path to it over dried
mud and rocks. She carries the precious sandals like a
wedding bouquet. Inside the old man's wives have their
houses, single-room houses, huts, neat, grass covered,
clothes drying, hung on bushes and sticks. Kids. So many
kids. Adedeji's mother greets her with a closed, sardonic
grin. She gestures for her to sit down on an awkward
chair, something that angles back in a way that
Gwendolyn can't possibly fit her body into. Someone
brings a stool and Gwendolyn settles onto it. Adedeji
tells her that she looks like a queen. People peer from
doorless houses, from behind trees. They gather behind
her, giggling, adolescent girls, cloths held tight over high
hard breasts and boys rushing around while Adedeji
heaps presents on them all.

The mother smiles open-mouthed this time. A tooth
is gone.

Gwendolyn smiles back.

Someone brings tea.

The hut they bring her to that night is dark. The bed
is iron—a spring on legs and a thin mattress made of
some dried grass. An earthen jug of water and a plastic
cup so old that dirt is imbedded in it are there on an
unsteady table. One of the young girls comes in with a
lantern, a bowl of rice, and a spoon. The rice has some

oily leaves and a few pieces of yellow meat on top of it. The girl stares at Gwendolyn with distrust, moving around her at the same distance. She pours some water and backs out of the hut. Gwendolyn cannot eat the stuff. She takes some papers out and tries to work. She gets out her novel, a mystery by Alistair MacLean. The lantern is too weak. She tries to drink some of the water but it's slimy and tastes of clay. The sheet on her bed is rough, washed in strong chemicals. The room smells of acid and insect spray. Gwendolyn had expected Adedeji would be there. She stretches out on the bed and waits.

In the morning Adedeji comes and tells her that he had to spend the night with his father and some friends in a nearby compound. "Gentlemen affairs," he says. "I will come to you tonight," he says, "but today I have more things to do. I own a few farms around here. Everyone will look after you."

He leaves her. His mothers and sisters (or whoever the hell they are) try to involve her in their work but she understands nothing of what is going on. One girl—a sister?—hovers around her more than the others with an intense curiosity that Gwendolyn knows is jealousy. The girl is tall and lean from hard work. She has deep brown skin and her hair is plaited in cornrows to the nape of her long neck, where it makes a delicate fringe. Her eyes, like Adedeji's, are ovals slanted back over high cheekbones. Her shoulders and back are narrow, angled down to a slender waist where her body curves out to a woman's hips and long dancer's legs.

After a long pantomime, it becomes clear that she wants to see Gwendolyn carry something on her head in the manner of a Yoruba woman. Gwendolyn removes her sandals to give it a try. She becomes the center of interest, her great, clumsy body swaying, her neck too weak, her hair a high pillow on which nothing will sit. The girl gestures, offering to plait Gwendolyn's hair.

The American's hair is soft and the African girl

makes a high, surprised sound when she touches it, calling the others over to feel it. They all come shyly with tentative fingers, giggling when they contact it and then running away with excited cries. The girl braids Gwendolyn's hair, standing back to admire her handiwork and then admiring Gwendolyn with awe. Finally she dares to poke the flesh around Gwendolyn's neck and presses a palm on the woman's large breast, smiling and nodding in approval and envy.

Gwendolyn tries the basket on her head again. They teach her the words: *Wa gbe ru mi.* "Come put it on my head." Funny nasal syllables. She laughs now, tipping nearly over and looking, she thinks, like a token in some Walt Disney film. The girl meanwhile has taken Gwendolyn's mighty shoes and is walking around on them, or trying to, as unsteadily as Gwendolyn with the basket of pineapples on her head. Everyone is laughing. A small boy rushes in and pushes the girl over. She falls on Gwendolyn and the two of them crumple in a heap of dust giggling like little kids.

The girl shows Gwendolyn some onions. Teaches her how to say it, *alubosa.* Makes it clear that Gwendolyn is supposed to cut these onions into slices and put them in this pot. She has a fire going and is boiling some yams and goat meat. Gwendolyn is frying the onions in red palm oil while her friend is tossing in hot peppers and demonstrating what they are going to do to Gwendolyn's mouth when she tastes them.

Then suddenly the girl grabs Gwendolyn's arm. "Adedeji!" she announces, smiling and nodding. The man steps through the gate and comes across the red compound. Huge. His shoulders are wide and the cloth of his great robe has golden threads woven into it, embroidered at the neck with spiraling gold symbols. He seems to float, shimmering in the red sun, glistening in the dusk.

"Is she your wife?" Gwendolyn asks him that night.

He sits in her dark hut fingering the lantern.

"Yes," he says.

"What did you bring me here for then, huh?" she asks.

"I wanted you to see my home, my family—"

"Your *wife?*"

"Not necessarily that, but you're American, black. I thought the village . . . the . . ."

"You were with her last night? Tonight me?"

"Look," he said, "it isn't that way here. You're using some ideas you bring from America. It's different in Africa."

"You think she doesn't know?"

"She knows. Of course she knows."

"You think she doesn't care?"

"That's another matter. It hasn't any relevance though. Besides, she's lucky. She knows I only plan to have one wife. She won't have to face—all this. My mother hated being the third wife. The first wife hates her. My wife won't have that."

"Oh, Jee-sus, and when do you, like, *plan* to get her out of all this? When do you take her to Lagos so you can't mess around? What's the difference between you and your old man is what I want to know? Except you're cheap. And I ain't about to be your second wife, you bastard," she says. "So get your black ass out of here."

She dusts her multicolored sandals, ties the heel straps together with a little bow she digs out of her purse, and takes them to Adedeji's wife. The young woman is hunkered alone by her fire stirring the soup she and Gwendolyn had made so happily that afternoon. Her feet are cracked and caked with ashes; ashes streak her face. (Have there been tears?)

Gwendolyn hands her the shoes. She doesn't understand at first but gets the picture and brightens. She dusts off her sorry-looking feet and puts the glorious sandals on, towering and strutting and smiling at Gwendolyn.

"Lookit 'em shoes!" Gwendolyn sings.

After that it wasn't so hard for Gwendolyn to get her work done. She swore off men. Mrs. Stegler got excited and helped the kid with some of the fine grammatical points of her paper and Gwendolyn, the scholar-nun, turned the thing into something she knew she was going to fly with. Title: "Cottage Industries in Polygamous Yoruba Households." Thesis: That Yoruba women produced all the goods and ran all the businesses in the rural areas of Western Nigeria and that any development efforts in the area should be focused on them and not their menfolk. She gave the paper in Washington at a World Bank seminar on Women in Development and was awarded a scholarship to attend courses at the Hague.

When she got home to Mississippi, her mother was in despair. Melchior was going to Boston, to that citadel of honkydom, Harvard University ("I cain't even pronounc't it," she said) on a very big scholarship. She was sure they would turn him into a cracker or one of them fancy niggers who marries white gals. When Gwendolyn muttered something about Holland, it seemed to be the end of everything. Mrs. Johnson shrieked, "Ain't *no* black folks in Holland. NONE!" She was standing there ironing Melchior's shirts to absolute perfection and she had sunk every penny she had into a new wardrobe for that boy.

"I bought you a new stove, Mamma, and an icebox," Gwendolyn said. But the woman was not talking.

Everyone stood around then and Gwendolyn started digging out presents. Bright cloths, afro combs, beads, a couple of batiks to hang on the walls, carvings of people who looked just like them, and a little black hand-sewn doll for her baby sister Louise who was already talking up a storm. In the rubble of the unpacked things, this little Louise finds a picture of her sister in Yoruba duds, and she stands there looking and holding the thing for awhile.

"Dat you, Gwind'lin!!!" she finally says. The little

girl gives a funny laugh like someone who is already used to trick photography, and then off the track says, "Hey, Gwind'lin, you gonna give me them bes' shoes I grows up? You gonna give me them hi' hi' shoes?"

"I don't have them shoes no more," Gwendolyn tells her. "I already give them to someone over in Africa. Someone who didn't have no shoes atall."

"It far 'way, ain't it?" says the little kid. "Someplace far 'way like Mamma say?"

"Jest 'bout as far 'way as you can git."

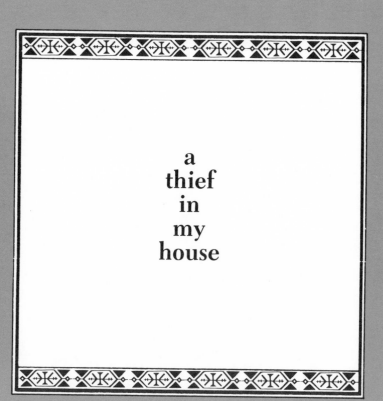

a
thief
in
my
house

Not more than fifteen minutes ago I took a bath, but either because of the wicked African heat or because of my nerves, I can already smell the sweat in my armpits. Listen, I don't shave there anymore; although sometimes, if I'm fiddling around with scissors, I reach around and trim a little. And since I'm left handed, see, I do a better job on the right side. I didn't stop shaving under my arms because of any women's lib, either. I stopped because I had this Mexican boyfriend who told me how he loved the hair under a woman's arms and on her legs. But listen, I still shave the legs.

My husband Allen noticed when I stopped shaving and complained. I told him I'd shave under my arms as soon as *he* did. He threatened to stop shaving his face, so I said as soon as I started to grow a beard, I would shave *that* if he wanted. Maybe I shouldn't have said anything, because now I'm getting these hairs on my chin and on the edges of my mouth and I have to pluck them constantly.

My husband Al makes a big salary but he's stupid. I wrote all his papers in college. Then I wrote the application letters each time he went for a job. I fill out all his forms and keep all his records. Sometimes I think the man can't read. I really feel like it's my job and I should get the money. But he has the degree (my degree). I never went to college. It bothers me, but as my friend Barbara said once, "Shit, Julie, you can run a farm—put in a whole day on a tractor. People went to college can't always do that!"

Al and I had this farm once. He's older than I am and I met him at a state fair with some cattle I raised—Angus. They called him "cradle-robber" when we started going out and his wife, Sue, tried to kill me. That was long ago. Now we have two kids and everyone thinks we're the same age. I have to admit I'm not aging well, and he's too dumb to worry about anything, so he looks great. If you like the type.

You never get used to the heat in the tropics. Each year I feel it more. Even with the air conditioners on, I'm always damp under my arms and between my legs. Under my breasts, tiny rivers form and trickle to my waist. Even though I wear sandals most of the time, my feet are always wet, so the dirt collects between my toes and cakes there. We all make lots of money but no one likes it here. We tell each other horror stories. Muriel Phillips had a dog that got squeezed to death by a boa constrictor in her backyard. Annie Jones had an emergency operation for a kidney stone but she really had an ulcer. Everyone has little stripes of shit running down the backs of their toilets because we all have dysentery.

Al travels a lot and I'm alone a lot. He did this when he was an extension agent back in Oklahoma. Once, when he was gone, I got this idea there was a thief in my house. My supplies of bouillon cubes seemed to be going down faster than they should, and each morning I had to look at the milk bottle to see how much had been taken during the night. The sugar was disappearing. I was always buying bread.

"I think my kid is stealing my butts," I told Al Junior's fourth-grade teacher. "Watch him at recess and tell me, huh?" The teacher was this thin guy with glasses, red eyes, and pale gray hair. When I was with him, I pretended I liked poetry and I learned to play old English ballads on my guitar for him. Then he came to me one day and said, "I'm getting transferred."

But it was only to a school four miles down the road. I think the bastard took some of my towels because I noticed the stack in the linen closet was smaller. After him, it was easy enough to meet others. I just started hitting the bars.

Sometimes I look at my daughter Maggie and wonder whose kid she really is, but that's just to torture myself. She's Al's all right. The result of a couple nights he spent at home. Al still travels most of the time. But now, folks, he ain't some lowly extension agent poking around the dogies in Oklahoma. Now he is an agricultural expert. A big-time *overs*eas *ex*patriate adviser. My Al.

"Ferrin' service," his old man says and roars laughing. I travel around with the expert sometimes, because I like to see things and learn things and because, like I say, I'm the one who writes up his reports. He takes them over to the office and they get typed up by the secretary there and then he brings them home. All neat. All spelled right. Only it makes me sick: it's his name on them.

I think I'll have to wash under my arms again. Then I'll drive over to Don's flat with my bottle and I'll be there when he gets back from work. I'll be drunk by the time he gets there. By then I'll probably look awful. I hate to think about it. I've made sure that my hair is clean and cream-rinsed and I used a little henna to put some color back into it. I rubbed my skin with scented oil and kind of smudged the eye makeup under my eyes the way the Indian women do. The mysterious look. I even try to pretend that I don't have freckles. But I know that after I drink, the blood rushes to my face and I look splotchy. My eyes get vacant and pathetic and my hair turns dry and staring. I've seen it in the mirror.

Last time I was at Don's he tried to get his key back from me. He said it was all over. I told him that I only wanted his friendship anyway, and a place to stay when I couldn't be alone anymore, but he knows this isn't true. He knows I want to get him back from Helga. She took him away from me. Just like that. Listen, the irony is too much: didn't I fix them up?

I met Helga on the beach. Her body was better than mine and she was younger. Her hair was styled in a European way. She was German, just divorced, visiting a brother who worked for Lufthansa. I invited her over, pretended to fix her up with Don in case Al was suspicious and to show Don that I wasn't afraid of losing him. I never thought they would start anything. For one thing, she's German. How can an American go for a foreigner, that's what I thought. I was that dumb.

"Helga's pregnant," he tells me. "She's coming back here so we can get married." His hair is turning gray. Creases are growing around his neck. I try to focus, hoping my lipstick is still there, but I can see that in the heat I have unhooked my bra and my tits are drooping under the puckering cloth. Why did I wear this shitty jersey anyway? I show him my new ivory bracelet. Don. He's moving, fixing coffee for me.

"What about us?" I say. Somehow I'm sitting at the table smiling, smelling his after-shave lotion. Should I try to hook it? The bra?

"Don't worry," he says.

That night a scorpion bites the gardener's boy. I call Don. He comes over right away. We take the kid to the hospital. The gardener wants to take the kid to a witch doctor but I shout at him.

"The kid's saliva is *black*," I tell Don. "I'm scared."

We come back to my place and drink brandy and I hate to admit it, but I beg him for it.

Okay, the maid sees Don there in my bed in the

morning. She stands smiling at the sink when I come out. I estimate that she has eaten about three slices of my bread already, probably with some jam, which she has carefully put back into the fridge. I always wondered if I should tell her that I know she's taking things from me. Now I'll have to hold back: she has something on me.

"Cook the breakfast!" I yell and then stop, saying, "hello," in her own language, softening my voice. I don't want her to hurt me. She fixes two cups of coffee.

The gardener's son is standing at the window. He has amulets tied around his neck—tiny horns of some small antelope. On his wrists are little pouches of powder and his ankles are painted red.

"Where did you get the money to buy this shit?" I shout to the gardener, dragging the kid over to him. "Don't think it isn't expensive!"

"Memsaab, I . . ." is all he can say.

"Have you let this man in the house so he can steal my money?" I ask the maid.

"I don't know," she says. I storm away from them.

If I told Don over our breakfast, what would he say? If I said to him what I've wanted to say—"Listen, Don, Allen Junior likes to stick his fingers up inside little girls,"—would he tell me what to do about it? Would he tell me it wasn't my fault? Would he tell me it would pass? But the kid's already sixteen and so they'll probably lock him up.

When you live overseas, you're supposed to entertain. You're supposed to welcome everyone who arrives and give going-away parties for everyone who leaves. When I got here, I thought, yes, yes, I'll do everything I'm supposed to. I bought fifty cheap porcelain dishes and we had big parties. But now, listen to this, I've only got thirty-one of those dishes left!

"Everything must be growing legs and walking

away," I told Big Al. "When it gets down to twenty dishes," I said, "no more parties. I mean it."

Sometimes I read other people's mail. Not all the time. Only to find out things. I saw Roy Carlyle's pay-slip envelope on Al's desk one day. So I opened it. It was just as I thought. That weiner Carlyle was making more money than Al (than me). So I went over to Mary Carlyle's house. My neck was flaming red. I hadn't brushed my hair. She offered me coffee. I said, "Give me whiskey!" I said, "When are *you* going to start having some parties around here, doll?" and she was so startled that her foolish pink eyes crossed. "Surely *you* can afford it more than we can, Mary," I said. In her silver tray I saw how swollen my eyes looked. Only slits remained.

She said, "What are you talking about?"

"I'm talking about thirty-two grand a year," I said, "and about the stupid fool I've been."

At Don's today I rip open a letter from Helga right in front of his face and start reading it out loud. He looks sick. Yeah, she's pregnant all right, but it sounds like a deal they cooked up just to get rid of me. The bitch. And after I gave her that blue silk jumpsuit I bought in Paris on the way out here. She thanked me for it by "borrowing" my Chanel No. 22 and never giving it back. I could have told Don right then, "She's a kleptomaniac," but I kept it to myself. I can smell the Chanel on the envelope.

"Why do you think I came over here?" I ask him. Don looks pale, soft, like someone who is puffing himself to a cloud. The only thing I can see is the big silver buckle on his trousers. In my hand is a telegram from the American embassy in Nairobi, Kenya. It says: MEET ALLEN WILCOX JR. ALITALIA FLIGHT 402 FROM NAIROBI STOP SCHOOL PROBLEMS REPORT FOLLOWS.

"Report follows," I tell Don, tell his belt buckle, tell the roll of fat that is starting to push over it.

"Is it marijuana?" he says.

"Try child molesting," I say.

"But he's a child himself," he says.

"Give me whiskey," I tell him. "He ain't no child."

When I took Maggie out of her crib some seven years ago, I hated her because she had grown up. I told Al, "All the babies are gone now," and he said something about how I wasn't such a baby lover that he ever noticed. But I was. I was twenty-seven then and the booze was already starting to show on my face.

Peg Simpson came one day and told me about Al Junior and her little girl. I said I didn't believe her. She came in with her large dark eyes and her soft good ways. She took some coffee with me and said things like, "I think you ought to know." She was kind and concerned. "Frightened," she said. For me and Al, for Al Junior and Maggie. I told her that her kid was a bratty little liar who had some words put into her mouth by her dirty-minded parents. I told her to fuck off.

She said, "If you refuse to admit it, then I'll have to warn everyone with small children about him. I have no choice." I told her to stuff it. But listen, this was no big news to me. When we came to Africa they told us we could send our kids away to school. All paid for. Fine, I thought. Good. Let someone else handle it. This was no big news to me. I had a little girl once, too, didn't I? She was six when Al Junior was twelve. About six, like Rebecca Simpson.

Don is at the stove fixing me something to eat. He's a good cook. I can smell the onions just starting to fry. He touches them gently, with the burner turned way down, a pale blue flame circling under the pan. Sweet onions melting like sugar.

"Sit here, Julie, I'll fix you something nice and then I'll take you home." Look, there is nothing worse than the tone in his voice when he said that. Nothing. Like someone gave you the wrong present and is trying to get it back. It was the very thing you wanted. And he meant it for someone else. And he doesn't want you to know who. Helga.

"Go meet the plane, will you, Don? I'll go home and never come back here if you just go meet that plane."

"Okay, Julie. Sure, Julie, I'll meet the kid. His father's out of town, so I'll meet him. Don't worry. Only don't tell me about it; don't tell me what he did."

"Let the little pervert take the fucking bus home then if you won't hear about it."

"But what has that got to do with . . ."

"Don't go to the plane!" I said. The man looks like lard in a plastic bag.

"Someone should go meet him," he says.

"Well, it ain't gonna be me," I tell him. He looks so bewildered. I want to throw a big one at him. I want to tell him that when Big Al gets back, I'm telling everyone about us. I want to ask him if he'll take me instead of that Kraut.

"How can you love someone that doesn't speak your own language? I just want to know. No reason. Just curious."

"Julie," he says, "what are you starting now? You mean Helga? Helga speaks Engl . . ."

"MAN, OH, MAN are you stupid!" I shout. "HELGA SPEAKS ENGLISH. Helga speaks. Helga Helga Helga . . ." (I'm thinking how come he doesn't just walk away from me like Big Al does.) "You think I'm talking about fucking English? Is that what you think I'm talking about?"

"But you asked me . . ."

"Man," I laugh. "Let Helga have you. Jeeeesus." He's putting some pieces of fish in with the onions. Fish that he's been soaking in lemon juice. Fish he's sprinkling with pepper.

"What time does the plane get in?" he asks me.

"Never. I want to see the kid walk, see? *Walk*."

Big Al doesn't know. He knows that he doesn't like

the kid. He knows that he doesn't like me. He knows that
he doesn't like Maggie. Sometimes, before I offer to help
him with his work, I sit watching him at his desk with his
legs crossed, hunched over his writing pad like he's trying to take a crap. Shit might come out of him but no
words ever do. I watch his red face, his white knuckles,
and his small eyes. Oh, he would never ask me. He only
waits until I'm ready. Now suppose I'm knitting. He
knows what my knitting is—I have never ever finished a
single thing except one sock for Al Junior about three
years ago—and he fumes while I click the little needles
away to my own tune.

My sister, Janette, said, "Don't marry him, Julie.
You're only eighteen. Don't do it. You'll be stuck someplace doing nothing, going no place." She was wrong. I
read the papers and the want ads. I got us off that damn
farm. I found out what I wanted and I plugged that man in
just like a light socket. A light I could see the world with. I
had him ready when the time came. He had his degree.
He had his experience. He got the job. My job.

But somehow, coming to Africa was a big mistake.
Maggie's gone to a boarding school. Al Junior is worse
now, lower now. Big Al travels constantly so he won't have
to face anyone and talk. I can write his papers, but he has
to talk for himself. Then he's silent, hiding behind his
quietness, hoping no one will notice. I'm alone. My
mirror tells me time is robbing me. Each day a little more
is gone. Al and I still screw, but I don't come anymore. It's
like someone is stealing the parts of my body that feel.

"Listen," I tell Don, my listener, my audience who is
just about to quit the theater along with the others.
"Listen, he's not a bad kid. Maybe there is something we
can do to help." Just what the old boy wants to hear. He
starts rattling off suggestions. Shrinks. Understanding.
Love. When he was a baby, I loved him. How I loved and
loved and loved him. No mother ever loved a kid the way
I loved that one.

"What did I do wrong?" I ask Don. His fish has been served to me with some lettuce and tomato. A sprig of parsley. I'm getting sober. I ask Don this question because there isn't a chance in hell that he will have an answer.

"Perhaps his father traveling so much . . ."

"Yes, maybe," I say tasting the fish, tart with lemon, the spiced pepper biting my tongue. "And maybe," I go sweet as apple pie, "it was his drunken whore of a mother always on the make. Is that what you think?" Poor old Don looks so shocked, hardly knowing what to say.

I hate this place. A sick breeze rank with low tide blows hot through Don's flat. Yesterday there was a green snake in the bathroom, coiled in the sink. It was thin enough to have come up in the drain but not smart enough to get out the same way. It looked at me with disdain. Over the towel rack I saw it had deposited its old skin. There it hung, transparent but still etched with the memory of its old markings, what it once had been. I knew that when the last bit of moisture dried from the skin, it would crumble. I hate it here.

Don is giving me coffee. He's saying, "Julie, let's go together to meet the plane. It will show him we care about him. We can't just let him . . ."

"So you *do* want me to tell you then?"

He says, "Can't he tell it? I'm willing to be his friend."

"You think for one minute that that freak will tell you anything? Dream on."

"His father has ignor . . ."

". . . is ignorant, is an ignoramus. You might as well say it."

"I didn't say that." Is it possible, I wonder, to push this mild man to his very limit? How far is it to his edge? How far to mine?

"And when Helga gets here, then will you be his friend? Doesn't she have a kid? Wasn't she married? Isn't it a little *girl?* Will you be his friend then? Will you be *mine*, more to the point."

"Yes, of course, I want you to be if . . ."

"Jeesus, are you dumb," I say. "Just give me some whiskey."

The clock over the stove in Don's flat tells me that, unless it was delayed, the plane from Nairobi has landed. It tells me that my son with his sixteen years is standing hunched and dirty in the customs line with his awful hair tucked up under a hat so the authorities won't see it. His front tooth is chipped and dying. I want him to get it fixed, but he refuses. He is taller than I am. How can I ever forgive him for that? He looks at me with my own blue eyes, his nose is my nose, his lean hands, my hands. There was a time when I could have held him in my arms as much as I wanted, whenever I wanted, but now he's too tall.

I have written a letter to Big Al. It says, "You can tell by looking at this kid, at the striking resemblance to his mother, that you had very little to do with it. Let's just continue along these lines for the time being. Leave us alone."

The whiskey comes at me with a flash, a hot rush, even after Don's good food. Through its blur, my fierce headache and the blaze on my face, I see my pal and neighbor here, Peggy Simpson, mother of a molested child, standing over me.

"Your son Allen is home," she says. "Locked out. Look, Julie," she says, "forgive me, but I can't look at him. Julie, I'm not like this, you know it. I don't want to be like this. Please. He's sitting in my living room waiting. How can I let him stay there?" Her good eyes bathe me.

"You're absolutely right. He can't stay there," I say, taking her damp hand. "The little bastard is a thief. He's been stealing things from me since day one. From me, his own mother."

silver
sugar
from
bombay

The woman wants to go to Canada but she has no passport and no way of getting one. She can't get out of Tanzania without one and she can't, obviously, get into Canada without one either. "Why is the world like this?" she asks. "It's a terrible problem. They say I am not a citizen. Maybe I am not a human being?" She has a cloudy and drifting eye and a habit of tugging on her sari. The thin cloth flutters nervous answers to her questions: all negative. "If I was not born here, how did I come here?" She claims there is no record of her immigration, no previous citizenship to hang onto. "I was inside my mother's body is the reason why." Worse yet, there is no record of her birth. "They forgot to register," she explains. "But I was born, I assure you." This is not said as a joke: her bad eye is glazed with tears like egg in aspic.

The woman with her clucks in sympathy. She stirs (I count them) five heaping teaspoons of sugar into her tea. Delicately, she pours a little into a saucer, making room. She has pushed her cakes away: gaudy, awful things iced in pink and green. Everyone knows these cakes are not made with butter. "Toooooooooo sveeeeet!" the woman giggles. A black waiter who's been watching moves in for the cakes, but she stays his hand. "No!" she tells him. "*Hapana chukwa.*" Pulled tight as elastic, the sari edge presses into the proud folds of brown flesh at her waist.

Her fat is no worry. "Oh, such a bad taste!" she says. "What do they use in them?" She dabs her mouth with a napkin.

I watch them and eavesdrop, impolite as it is. They either don't notice or don't care. We're all in this together, nothing to do, lingering over tea at the hotel.

"I went to the Indian High Commission. They asked me, 'Are you Indian citizen?' Look what you see, I told them. You see an Indian, isn't it? They only want to see papers."

"What to do? What to do?" the other asks. She's managed to eat the cakes and is pouring more tea. Her moving arm stirs the fat at her midriff, opens deep creases of secret stuff there, rich, dark, and oily, and on the swell of it a bloom of peach, rolls like chocolate butter frosting on pink angel cake.

"When I went to the Tanzanians, they are also asking if I am citizen. Where is your visa? Where are your working papers? But will they believe it?"

"They cannot believe," says the other one, beefing up the tea with spoon after spoon of sugar. "Ack, this sugar is no good. Look how dirty!"

"They are telling me I cannot work. If I cannot work, how do I live?"

"You cannot live."

The woman who wants to go to Canada is a resident at the hotel. Her room is next to mine. In the few days I've been here, I've noticed constant activity in there. Something is always going on in that room. Things break in there. Things go wrong. Already repairmen have been up three times to fix the air conditioner. The phone company has been around twice. Two painters arrived with buckets and brushes and stayed a few hours. Plumbers came: I heard the water running, the toilet flush. A carpenter showed up. I heard hammering. This morning, waiters from the hotel restaurant carted out a small

refrigerator and carted in another small refrigerator—a
newer one. The woman really lives in that room, a
resident.

The hotel, in fact, is full of people like her—Indians
who only look like Indians, who have no papers, no place
to go. The entire clientele goes under the same few
names—Singh, Patel, Chandra, Gandhi. Looking at the
register is like reading the aliases of the unimaginative or
the guest list at the reunion of some enormous biblical
family. It's an Indian exodus: they've sold their houses,
their belongings, and now they're waiting to get out,
waiting for visas to England, Canada, the United States.
They've seen some grim racial slurs in the handwriting
on the wall.

The two women finish their tea, fidget all that material around into the right places, and prepare for the
standing position. They smooth yards and yards of it into
straight pleats, fluted columns to the floor, flesh rolling
under it as they stand. Each one tosses a long, free end of
sari over a shoulder. The fluttering silks wave as if part of
the farewell ritual. "I will beg the Indian High Commission. I am Indian, you are only to look at me. Give me a
paper and I promise I won't go to India . . ." passing heavily behind me then on the way out, their perfumes and
the soft push of their cloths. Long, thick braids trail
across the back of my chair.

Her name is Leela and she's a Patel. We see each
other in the hall and restaurant so often that we finally
have to speak. To tell the truth, I was trying to avoid it.
Could it be that in the short time since I have been here,
I've picked up the East African aversion to these people
from India? They call them "Asians" around here and it's
not a very nice word, removes them handily to the East
but doesn't really locate them any place special. A lump-
ugly word, it strips them of their origins, their countries,
their languages, their ways. "Asians," as though someone
decided long ago that they didn't belong anywhere and

never would. Even to me, they seemed an intrusion in Africa.

It's awful to say this, but at first these brown people seemed like exotic curiosities and tourist attractions, rather than real honest-to-God human beings. Hadn't Leela herself asked the question: "Maybe I am not a human being?" Maybe it was the clothes they wore, the jewelry, their extraordinary wealth of hair, the eye makeup, the dots on their foreheads and the rings in their noses. Maybe it was the incredible food they ate: it came in such outlandish colors, smelled of such a confusion of spices. Everything about them was rococo, like decorations on an outrageous monument. Even their English flipped and spun and trilled beyond baroque. And they led such elaborate, teeming lives. Every morning their kids poured down into the hotel restaurant for breakfast like a warning sequence from a film pushing birth control. And their fathers all the same, walking about in a mood of mechanized seriousness, as hard and deliberate as machines, while their mothers all buzzed like summer gardens. They seemed churned out past individuality, past problems, past emotion.

Africans seemed more real to me. After all, they were the people I had expected. Besides, I had grown up looking at black faces all my life. I certainly did not grow up looking at women who wrapped themselves in yards and yards of silk, put bright dots on their foreheads and rings in their noses. Or men who wore flapping pajamas or enormous diapers. Or men, the Sikhs, who never cut their hair or shaved their beards but rolled it all, tied under turbans, the beard in two tight twists like basket handles choking under their chins and up their cheeks. One day, on the street, a turban fell to the wind and the Sikh's hair never seemed to stop, a thin slick rope of it, long, uncoiling, slithered like a snake, the tail of it on the ground as the Sikh arched and spun for the headdress, grabbed, sputtering and winding his hair again and again high on his head while the Africans stood around and laughed.

I heard stories of rapacious Asian materialism, about their hoards of wealth stuffed in mattresses or buried in the floors of their shops. The Africans plain want them to go away, but Asians are like a shameful addiction—no one is sure how it got started, how it got so out of hand, or how to kick the habit. Asians run everything, build everything, fix everything. Africans resent it and want to be cured, but cold turkey is no fun. When Idi Amin threw all his Asians out of Uganda, everything with a motor broke down, including the sugar-processing plant. East African scuttlebutt has it that these brown bastards took crucial little pieces from all the machines, pieces no African had known about, pieces the Asians had kept secret. When there was no more sugar for his troops, Amin ended up inviting a bunch of Pakistanis in to get things going again. And the Pakistanis came! Asians will go anywhere.

Leela is having a tea party in her room, to which I'm invited. She calls it "a professional ladies' tea" and it's on Saturday afternoon when everyone is off work. At the tea are Mrs. Singh, Mrs. Singh-Kalsi, Dr. Singh and her niece, Mrs. Bardyal-Singh, and two Mrs. Patels. There are two lawyers, an educator-writer, a medical doctor, an architect, and an economist. Leela introduces me around as a journalist. Everyone seems to have a profession, like a Sunday hat. I'm suspicious. I know my introduction is spurious and Leela, who's passing herself off as an accountant, is, I happen to know, a clerk at the local Peugeot dealer. Leela is convinced that I will have lots in common with Mrs. Singh (educator-writer) and sits me next to her. The woman is thin, frail, with very fair skin and hair too black. Her beautiful pink sari is embroidered with white and yellow flowers. She looks ready to expire, whispers to me, "I admire you very much for your work. A journalist! It must be very exciting. Are you covering a story here?"

I tell her, "I'm looking for a story."

She says, "It's too quiet here. Nothing happens. Isn't that so?"

Leela comes forth with a tray of teacups. Behind her one of the waiters from below brings a platter of savories that he places on her bureau. Everything looks crisp, fried balls and wedges; nothing has a real shape on that tray and most of it is in astonishing colors, the deep oranges and cadmiums of turmeric. There's an awesome smell of anise, cinnamon, cumin, of spices I have no names for, of rose waters and orange waters and the sharp tang of fresh ginger she's put in the tea.

Mrs. Singh (writer-educator on my left) tells me Leela has borrowed the kitchen of Mrs. Patel (lawyer) to make all this stuff. "This is not from the hotel kitchen!"

"Leela is a wonderful cook," Dr. Singh says. "My husband is always asking me when Leela is coming to cook for us. She makes such marvelous sambals."

Leela, giggling, tells me, "When my parents were alive we prepared the real vegetarian. In those days, we had sixteen, twenty different dishes on the table. You could get everything then."

They all nod. "It isn't so now," the lawyer says.

They all sigh. "You know," Leela tells me, offering the savories, "in those days we were easily getting a certain kind of silver paper. It is made of sugar in some way, silver sugar, but thin as paper, and we use it to wrap our sweets. So very beautiful and you can eat it, too. I like it too much. If I could just go to Bombay, then I would get some."

"I would get almonds!" the educator-writer tells me. She has a pink mark on her forehead to match her dress. Leela seems to have a red one. Sometimes Leela's is blue: sometimes she has none. I get the feeling somehow that it really isn't very professional to have one because no one else in here does. Then I discover I've got something in my mouth that's so wonderful I think I'll swoon. There's no telling what it is. If they can't get anything these days, what was it like before? I feel like an Alice who's tastebuds have just gone to the other side of the looking-glass.

Someone across the room is asking me how much mangoes cost in America. She needs to know before she emigrates.

"But no one is getting green cards for States these days," Mrs. Patel (economist) says. "We have been trying for three years."

"Three years is nothing!" Dr. Singh tells her. They all laugh.

"I don't think you can get mangoes in America," I tell them.

"You can get," Leela says. She's done research. "They are growing in Florida and West Indies. But expensive, I tell you. You can pay fifteen shillings for one!"

"Even here they are too expensive," the educator-writer tells me. "Two years ago it was only some pennies for one; now it can reach two shillings, two and a half."

They all shake their heads. The architect says, "You are all such silly geese."

I, meanwhile, have developed a sudden addiction to the things on the savory tray, like an unfortunate person who never knew she was an alcoholic until she took that first sip. So, after the tea is over, I hang around for more, on the pretense of helping Leela straighten up. We sit around for more tea and work on the tray.

"You know driving?" Leela asks; her cloudy eye drifts over, lands on me, and drifts away. "I mean car driving."

"Yes," I tell her. In my mouth something is having a violent reaction to the ginger in the tea. I'm wondering if it's a kind of orgasm.

"Do you think it will take me long time to learn?" she asks.

"No," I tell her.

"Even if I am having problems with my eye?" she adds. "Not blind, mind you!"

"I don't know. They would test you before they let you drive."

She leans toward me, holding her sari to her breast. It falls from her shoulder and touches my arm as though trying to get my attention from the savory tray. "I wish to go to Canada, you see. There I will buy a very fine car, a white one of the type which is having the top go down. I will learn this driving and go in the car to my brother's house. I will find it on the map, you see. I will go there in surprise. That," she says, leaning closer, "is why I wish to go to Canada. My brother is there."

"Your brother got a passport then?" I ask her.

She doesn't answer. Instead she says, "I was having to stay behind with my mother. She was too old and my father already dead. His business was totally lost. My mother told Dilip, 'You must go. There is nothing left for you in this place.' Dilip said, 'I will send for you soon.' But she knew she would never see him again. After she was dead, he sent a letter to me. 'I am married to a Canadian,' he told me. Is this so his mother would not know? Is it because he is ashamed of this marriage? It's better for Dilip, isn't it? Safer? But I know," she says, "he will not be sending for me."

"Even if he did send for you," I tell her, "you couldn't go because of this passport business."

"And also because of my father's money, you see. I have no way to take it from here." She leans back in her chair, her good eye on me, the other looking toward the window. Even though my mouth is still throbbing with pleasure, I feel sorry for her and sigh along in sympathy.

"But you can help me," she says. "In a small way. For me a help and for you also a help." I have no idea what's up. Surely she doesn't think I have an in at the American embassy and can get her some papers?

No, it isn't that. Leela's talking about black-market money. Instead of the official eight shillings on the dollar, she'll give me sixteen for cash and twenty for checks deposited in her bank account in Toronto. She tells me there's a man, an American very high up in the embassy, who cashes a check with her every two weeks. This is to convince me that it's perfectly all right. "It's the only way for me to take my money out," she pleads. "When nothing is left, I will become a refugee. I will go to U.N. and tell them to give me a country. Can you have a person in the world who does not have a country? It is too serious," she says. "Can they tell me to go sit in the sky?"

"I can think of worse places," I tell her.

In Dar es Salaam you can spend the whole day trying to buy a hairbrush. Someone stole mine. In a beauty parlor, a woman looks at me and says simply, as though she's talking about the weather, "You can't get one in all the country. They are finished. Why don't you just cut your hair?"

Leela's friend, Mrs. Singh (architect), finishing up an appointment, assures me it's true. "They finished two months ago," she says.

The beautician repeats her advice, "Better to cut off your hair and use a comb."

On the way out, Mrs. Singh says she thinks she has an old hairbrush that she will loan me until I can write to a friend in America and have one sent. "Maybe you can buy one from someone who is leaving, at a yard sale."

"Maybe I will just cut it off," I tell her. "And use a comb."

She changes the subject, "Leela tells me you are a very good friend to her these days. It's so very kind of you. Of course, as a journalist, you must be very busy."

"Not so busy right now," I tell her.

"But tell me," she says, "what do you think are

Leela's chances? Canada, the United States, isn't it all the same? Very difficult, isn't it?"

"But she has a brother there. That will help."

"Dilip?" She laughs. "He has married a Canadian girl. I trust his wife will not welcome Leela. It's not the same with you people, is it? What is a husband's sister to you? Something that you call in-law. Leela knows this, of course, but then, she has to have hope. She's quite alone, isn't she?"

"Why doesn't she stay here?" I ask the architect. "Her friends are here. She has a job."

"Oh, dear, dear!" she says laughing. "None of us can stay here much longer. It's quite impossible. But tell me, do you think Leela can get a job there?" She puts her hand on my wrist, "Yes, it would be better for her to stay, but it's impossible. She will lose everything. We all will." Her tone is flat, like glass, shining and transparent. "Some of us will be able to start over. We who have professions. But can Leela start over? I, myself, know the problems because I have been to the States. Leela does not know what color we are there." She lifts the hand, perfume of rose water, bright nails flash. "No, she does not know about that. Have I offended you?"

Leela lives up to the popular myth that Asians have mattresses stuffed with money. "If we put it in a bank here, they will count it; then they will make a tax and take it away from us," she tells me. Today Leela is wearing a long terrycloth bathrobe. Her hair is undone, miles of it beyond her hips, remembering its braid. The remains of a dot, like misplaced mascara, is on her forehead. She's coming apart. "Then if someone will be taking the money from the bank, they will say, What did you do with the money? What did you buy? Show us the receipt. No no no no, the bank is no place to put money." I've got a check for four hundred dollars that I am sending to her bank in Toronto and she's pulling out a wad of pink hundred-shilling notes from the false back of a bureau drawer. Last time she fetched them from the closet. The time before it really was her mattress. Nothing original. I imagine her moving the little stashes around.

"How much more have you got to go, Leela?" It looks to me that at this rate, she'll be dishing out money from this hotel room for the next twenty years.

"Too much." She smiles. She's looking sad today. Her face powder is the wrong shade, her eyes smudged with kohl. Her fat is melting. She's complaining that there's no hot water. On the phone to the desk, her voice high pitched, pattering English laced with Hindi. She moves, gestures like a hand puppet's, stiff and graceless. A human being. There's no question anymore.

"What do you think," she asks, "if I go to Canada with no money?"

"But you have money, Leela. In that bank in Toronto. They won't take it from you. I promise!" I laugh at her.

"I have some. Only a little."

"How much?" In the papers, I've been reading about sums in the millions. Asians with millions and millions of worthless shillings, smuggling them out at incredible rates, turning up in Geneva at forty to the dollar like wallpaper. "Tell me how much and I'll tell you how long you can live on it."

Nothing doing: she's already found out. "I can live one year, maybe two. But I need to get a job there. I can't go to Canada unless I can get this car. It's too expensive, isn't it?" She giggles—her white convertible, her fantasy, the key to some sister-in-law's heart.

Black plumbers come. They look like thugs. Barefoot. Dressed in rags. They carry pipes and fittings. Wrenches. They slip into her room without speaking; they know her well. I feel the presence of her hidden loot as if all the hiding places were suddenly transparent, glowing pink with shillings from within. I wonder why these men haven't come in the night to kill her and raid the trove. In the bathroom, they run the water, muttering, banging on the pipes.

"But there *is* hot water, Memsaab," the boss tells her.

She shrieks at them, "You are *stupid! All of you! Stupid idiots!*" She rushes past them into the bath. I hear the water and her yell, "Just feel it! *You stupid idiots!*"

They say nothing. Two of them have remained in the room with me, they look at each other and laugh silently. Shrugging, they walk away. In the bathroom I hear the head plumber tell her, "I will report it to the manager, Memsaab."

"You tell him to get it fixed, you idiot," she shouts, following him out, slamming the door after him. "There is not hot water," she tells me. But she doesn't invite me in to test it.

Oh, Leela, my Asian banker, sad friend and neighbor, you are never going to get out of here with your dough. There are no suitcases big enough for the hoard and if you turned it all to gold, you couldn't heft it. You've told me about your deals involving poached ivory, how they confiscated the tusks at the border. No one pinned anything on you, but you lost a lot. Fifty tusks were yours. And I know the price, five hundred dollars a tusk. What will you do with your great buried treasure? It buys you nothing that you want. No citizenship, no passport, no way out. Not even silver sugar from Bombay.

Wednesday morning, Aftab, the desk clerk, one of the three or four queers in town, is running in what appears to be more than his usual flap, waving the morning paper. "Look at this!" he tells me. The government of Tanzania is issuing new hundred-shilling notes. There's a picture of the old note crossed out and the new one with the president's somber face glowering out at the Asians, saying, "Ha ha ha, I've got you now." The transfer is going to take place during a single work week starting next Monday. At the end of that week, the old pink notes will no longer be legal tender. Anybody on the way to Geneva with his trunks jammed full of the stuff might as well have a bonfire. Anybody who's got his mattresses, false drawers, and hollowed-out books packed with it, might as well kiss the little secret good-bye.

I ask an African waiter the reason they are making the new notes. He tells me, "The old ones are wearing out. These are better ones." But an African businessman at the next table leans over and explains, "There is too much of our money in Kenya. The Kenyans have stolen it to sell to the tourists before they come here. In this way they are getting dollars and we are getting our old money back."

I see Leela now in the hallway with Aftab. She reads the paper and adjusts her sari which appears to have suffered its own shock and come loose. She walks slowly to my table.

"I will give you ten thousand to change for me . . ." she starts in.

"Oh, no, you won't either, Leela. I'm not going into the bank with any ten thousand shillings. They'd ask where I got it."

"You are American," she says. "I'm Asian. No, they won't ask you anything. I will give you twenty thousand."

"Leela, no! I can't do it."

"You can keep ten percent," she offers. She's talking into space, working on a deal. Even her opaque eye is alive today. "Twenty percent," she says. "A commission. Twenty-five."

"You take the money in, Leela. If they tax you, so what? At least you'll get something."

"If I take my shillings in, they will see who I am. They will know I have no papers. They will tell me I have stolen. They will put me in jail. . . ."

"No, they will not," I tell her.

"More than a million shillings," she leans over the table, "More than two."

She's got more than two million shillings stuffed into that room? "Okay. I'll take in a thousand," I offer. It sounds pathetically small. "But no more than two thousand. I still have seven hundred left from what you gave me before and no papers to show where that came from."

She doesn't answer, spreads some awful jam on her roll, bites it, and grumbles, "Always stale."

Everyone knows that on Monday, start of business, the chaos at the banks will close down everything else in town. Over the weekend, people from the towns where there are no banks started filtering into the capital, pretending that their pockets aren't full of cash and that their suitcases have only underwear in them. Worried and slightly pissed-off nomads who don't think much of this paper stuff anyway camped in the central market and caused a sanitation crisis—just another reminder that it's better to keep your assets in cattle instead of cash, just another proof that there's a bunch of fools running things in the towns. These guys are flashing little balled-up wads of rancid money pulled out of leather pouches. It looks a thousand years old, prehistoric, as though it's been printed on papyrus. It isn't even pink anymore. A lot of nomads want to exchange their smaller bills, too; they don't trust any of it. They don't understand anything about it.

But the Asians understand. Some of them have dared, brought suitcases full of money to the bank. They have the flat, drugged look of people facing the dull prospect of harassment. Everyone with more than fifty thousand shillings, they have been told, must register the exchange. It spells doom. They can only gamble on the salvage value, but the odds, as usual, favor the house. A tall man with a long beard, white pajamas, and a white turban is up there right now, a rumor spreads, changing over three million shillings. The women ahead of me in the line are telling the story and giggling. It's too long to wait. Never mind the heat: a very old black man behind me, who also has come with a big suitcase, leans on his son or grandson. He has that special dignity of the old in Africa, but below him, spreading around his sandals in a dark stain is the urine he could no longer hold. They close shop on Monday without coming near the end of the line.

It takes me three hours on Tuesday to get inside the bank with my seven thousand three hundred of Leela's. She talked me into it. It's so hectic and sweaty in there that no one bothers to question the sum. Leela, meanwhile, has hit the bank as many times as she thinks she can without being noticed, taking in a couple of thousand every time. She's even taking some of it up north by charter plane to hit the banks up there. Plus, she's got a few other people like me, on commission, but the time is short and the lines long and by the end of the week Leela hasn't even made a dent in her fortune.

I find her in her room, freshly showered, freshly decked in a purple sari, sitting quietly in a chair. Behind her on the floor, in tight bundles like bricks, a wall of hundred-shilling notes. Old ones. I feel so terrible I offer to give up my commission and hand over the three thousand.

"No, it's yours," she insists. There's an emotion in the room with us, a tension—I'm not sure what it is—a mixture, maybe, of ruin and relief. "They will tell you," she says, "about our people here. How we have stolen. This and that they will say. Now you may see for yourself what has been stolen." She smiles like a mathematician who has just proved a new hypothesis.

I hold her shillings out to her, but her hands remain fixed in her lap. She glances toward her bureau and I put them there. "My father was having seven trucks," she says. "He was carrying cargoes from the coast to the inside and from the inside to the coast. Little, little he put his money away. In sixty-eight, they took away his trucks. They took his buildings. They took his cargoes. 'But they cannot take this money,' he said." It's all part of her theory now, the simple axioms and the ironic twist here at the end, shooting holes in the logic, declaring a new, terrible order. "Tell me, do you believe the dead can know what is going on?"

"Yes, I do," I tell her. "But I don't think they care."

She smiles broadly. "Of course," she laughs, "how is it they can care?"

Very soon I get a chance to leave the hotel and move into a house. Just before I am to leave, Leela borrows Mrs. Patel's kitchen and does a vegetarian lunch with more than twelve dishes and plenty of my favorites—Leela's mango pickle, something that tastes like a cross between green olives, jalapeño peppers, unripe Georgia peaches, and raw sauerkraut smothered in garlic. The luncheon is in honor of Dr. Singh, who has finally gotten green cards for all the family and will soon go to America. They have been waiting for almost five years.

It's the professional ladies again and despite the recent upheaval with the currency, which I am sure has hit them all in one way or another, they all seem much the same. They sigh about the dirty trick but they don't complain—a characteristic of the persecuted. The architect says she had been expecting it.

"Of course it was the only thing they could do," she says. "And in many ways, it was our own fault." She turns to me. "They believe our people don't trust their banks, that we want to hide things from them. And they are one hundred percent correct. If our people wish to stay here, they will have to change their ways."

Everyone nods. But, of course, everyone wants to leave, so no one is planning to change. Leela has served up a little cocktail of tamarind juice before the lunch and is clinking the glasses to make a toast. "We are here to say good-bye to Dr. Singh, who has been a kind and good friend to us all." We all look at Dr. Singh, raise our glasses, and sip. The tamarind is as bittersweet as the party. Mrs. Singh, the educator-writer, whose place seems permanently next to mine, whispers, "She has saved my daughter's life from typhoid."

"And I wish to tell you also," Leela goes on, "that I will soon get papers!" The little gathering goes silent.

"What? Leela!" the architect says.

Leela says, "I have told the U.N. I am refugee. They do not know from which place I am refugee." She laughs. "But they say if Tanzania does not give me a visa, I will have no place to go—same as a refugee. They wrote all this down."

"Will they send you to India?" Mrs. Patel asks.

"How," she asks, "when I am not Indian?"

"But the Tanzanians will give you a visa to stay," someone suggests.

"They have refused!" Leela says, like a person who's been tied up and has just gotten the last knot undone.

I tell her, "Perhaps they will make you sit in the sky." The women look puzzled. Leela nods, fixes her sari: her clouded, drifting eye relaxes and smiles along with the other one. "It's not such a bad place up there," I tell everyone. "You can get *everything*, even silver sugar, and you just have to wait for a good spot to jump off."

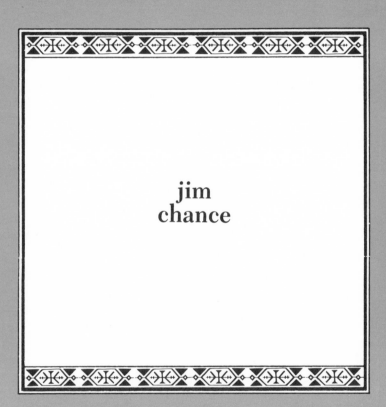

jim
chance

Christine saw them first, an unusual gathering, about fifty hippo just north of camp, lolling in the morning light before the sun rounded the high bank and drove them into the water, their skins iridescent pink.

"Like bloody cartoon characters," Jim Chance said. He remembered Disney's *Fantasia*, the hippo dancing around on toe shoes, a great joke. To him they were exactly that absurd. Christine figured that this was because they weren't predators or because he couldn't confront them on land, chase them down, dare them with guns. "Just don't get between one of those big suckers and the bloody river." He said *bloody* with something like a Texas accent, though he came from Connecticut.

He left her there alone then so she could draw freely, but in fact, she never drew animals and it amused her that Chance didn't know this. He assumed that like all the other prissy-ass artists who bugged the shit out of him with their pretty lion pictures, she had come to do the same. No. Her subject was tropical plant life and lately, the baobab trees that grew to enormous size here in the swamps with their twisted heavy trunks and stunted branches said to be their roots. The devil's tree, a story went, that had offended God and been turned over, its real branches doomed to hell. Baobabs were reservoirs of water on the plains and in times of drought elephants destroyed them, but here in the swamps, they were left to reach great age, seemed more a part of the earth's rock crust, except for the tortured forms they took.

Chance never asked to see what she did, never opened her sketch pads to peek, and never came around behind her as she worked, the way almost everyone else would do simply out of curiosity. He didn't care, wrapped in his own postures, his campaigns against poachers, his years in the bush, his frustrations with the Africans. He liked it best when he could confront something dangerous. She had seen him walk right toward a bull elephant to provoke a charge and then stand laughing as the elephant trumpeted and stopped inches from him, telling her that if she knew anything about elephants, she'd have known they wouldn't come over logs like that—"You didn't notice the log. You wouldn't. But I knew it was there." She wondered why he gave away the trick, to deflate his dare and expose everything else he did as a sham, but she decided it must have been because he wanted her to know how easily she had been fooled, one more dimension to his endless game.

He had a woman in town, Arlette, French and years older than he was, though it would have been hard to say how old Chance was. His skin had been ruined by the sun, almost deliberately, and he had the angry walk of a man with a steel pin in his back from an old football injury, the knotty used body of a former athlete. Christine decided that his ego was still adolescent and this did something to his expression: he could have been nineteen. He had never played football. He told her right away. He had hurt his back falling from a horse, he said, but later she overheard him tell someone else that a horse had trampled him, and though the lie was insignificant, it put another label on him for her.

The first time Christine had come to the Selous,

Chance's woman was with him. She slept in the back of the Land Rover with an aromatic plaster of oils and clay over her face and she left Christine up front to listen to Chance.

He told her, "You're bloody lucky to come down here. Not many white women do. Mostly they want the game parks. Disneyland. Open-air zoos. Six bloody tourist buses up every lion's backside. Listen, you don't see any lions down here unless you're bloody lucky and damn quiet. Why? Because they *run away.* That's why. Because they are *w-i-l-d.*" He laughed.

Christine was silent, almost entertained; he was such a type. She judged him to be the kind of man whose adventures taught him nothing, an identity pinned on tricks and dares and quick getaways. Even as he got to annoy her more and more later on, she put up with it because by then the place had captured her. And, of course, there were the baobab trees. Chance showed her one in a grove near camp, sixteen hundred years old, he said, maybe older. In the trunk was a deep cave, big enough for the two of them. Its bark was dense and cracked, its branches hung with weird flowers that opened at night. But it was the deep center full of water that attracted her, secrets her drawing went after but never reached.

All along the way, police knew Jim Chance. They let him through roadblocks with a wave. Only because, he explained, he had paid them off in advance. Hissing and booing past them, he told her, "They're all corrupt. People can say we did it to them, you know, the evil white man and all that shit. The innocent African. Well, I've seen enough *watu* (people, that is, Africans) who never saw a *mzungu* (a white man) and they're as corrupt as the next guy. You draw your own conclusions. Hell, you want to know what it takes to get a tusk past one of those guys? Twenty bucks. I'm talking about greenbacks, not your useless bloody shillings. Twenty greenbacks and you

could walk out with the goddamn thing in your mouth—
tell them it's a bloody false tooth."

It didn't bother Christine that he translated the
Swahili that way, patronizing her when she was almost
fluent in the language. He didn't know, but still, it made
him sound all the more ridiculous, this man, she thought,
driving too fast to show off and for whom? Not me, I'm
not impressed, just bounced to death. Arlette was sighing, rolling over: her perfume, vaporized, hung like a
haze in the car.

"Where's the next *rushua* coming from? The next
bribe," Chance went on, "this is all they want to know.
Who's got some tusks buried that they want to smuggle
out? Listen, they don't ask me to run their bloody *pembe*
out for them. I'm the one who caught up to every poach-
ing gang in this area."

"Jim's going to make a book from it," Arlette said
from behind. Her perfume was starting to fail. You could
smell her flesh in the hot car.

Chance said, "I've got pictures of the whole operation from A to Zed. I've got one of these guys actually
moving tusks through a bloody roadblock. No one else in
the world has pictures like these. *National Geographic*
wanted to buy them but I said no, not unless you buy the
whole damn book." Later he would talk about his book as
if it had already been printed, comparing it to the other
books on wildlife that were around. He was obviously
jealous of the other books, as though something had
been stolen from him and, perhaps on this account, he
wouldn't let anyone who came to the camp take his picture, or if one did, he'd grow angry and find a way to get
the camera and expose the film. In spite, Christine had
started to draw him, but as a cartoon character, puffed up
and grotesque: in one frame he was stepping on an elephant. Sometimes, though, she drew his body as it was,
square and muscular, and this aroused her and she

wanted to sleep with him: Which she thought interesting if not bizarre.

Villages had trickled away as they entered the reserve. The children along the way who ran out to the road to wave had disappeared. All signs of people dwindled. Then there was only bush. Perhaps it was imagination, but Christine thought, as they entered the Selous, that the air changed, as though it didn't belong to humans any longer and she could be charged somehow for what she used.

Chance announced, "Ladies and gents, the biggest game reserve in the world! Thousands of acres of Africa. We offer seven rivers, swamps, savannas, mountain ranges. This is the heart, the belly, the guts of the continent!" A carnival voice, but he got no laughs, not even from Arlette, who was sitting up by then, removing the oil from her face, combing her hair. She offered everyone scented towelettes in packets, smiling like an airline stewardess when the plane has landed safely.

"Oh, how I hate that ride," she said. She looked pale, too slim, improbable as the lover of such an outrageous man.

Chance said, "Now don't make any mistake, this is not some prissy-ass game park with your old ladies' lodge, everyone around with a martini and a tray of bloody horses' ovaries at sundown. Tickle a leopard under the chin like some pussy cat. Tell her what happens with leopards down here, Arlette."

"Ah, this leopard," she said, "he jumped down from a tree and this poor fellow, Carl, was underneath him taking pictures. The leopard took Carl's scalp with a claw. . . ."

"Tore the bloody thing right off," Chance said. "It was lying on the ground."

"Jim shot his gun in the air and the leopard was gone. Vanish!"

"I picked up this character's scalp, see, and put it

back on. Tied it there with my bloody undershirt. We got him in a helicopter and flew him to a doc in Nairobi. That's the kind of leopard we have here. You're not ready to walk with them, live with them, forget it, don't come down to the Selous. That's the way it is. We don't go around in armored vehicles."

Arlette touched Christine's arm. "It was a miracle after all; they stitched it back on. You didn't even see the scar under the hair." As if she were trying to reassure.

That first time Christine had made only a few drawings, but she knew right away that the place had material for her. She liked the eerie landscape full of danger and the swamps broken by silver strands of river. And the scale, everything so vast. There were enormous palm trees, a unique species that grew fifty or sixty feet tall. As the swamps shifted, filled and drained, some of the palms had died and lost their crowns, but the trunks remained, like avenues of ancient pillars holding up the sky. There were forests of baobab and on the high ground, huge cactus and the bleached white pods of thorn bush whistling in the wind.

Years ago, she would never have imagined herself doing this in some wild part of Africa, staying like a recluse in a tent, drawing funny trees. A city girl, she only did portraits and had a lifelong plan to draw a fixed set of subjects relentlessly as they changed and grew older, pressing, she hoped, to their very natures. She had several shows in D.C. but then got hepatitis and was sick and despondent for more than a year with no energy to work, and when she finally returned, she found her talent was gone. When she tried to draw again, her portraits were damned—that was the way she felt about them, damned, because she couldn't shake off the sensation that her subjects would all die. It made her cold when she took her pencil, to stand immobilized in front of blank sheets of paper. It was a terrible time in her life because there was nothing else she could do except draw. She waitressed for a while and saved her money and went to Africa where her cousin taught at a university. So she could change the scene, she told everyone at home; to get my shit together, she said.

Sometimes Christine had to pay dearly for her art. Chance liked to go out on game runs at sundown to see what he called "the Real Africa." She dreaded the times he would ask her to come with him, but worried too much about staying on good terms with him to say no when there was no one else at camp or when he seemed on edge. Afraid he might get hostile and tell her not to come back, or that he would sulk, or yell at her the way he yelled at Mugo, their cook. She feared he might try to charge her the rate he got for regular guests, which would have made her continued trips impossible.

It was always the same. They would drive from the river to where a high plateau dropped in a long sweep into a sickle-shaped valley full of buffalo. Each time, the car would stop on the rise as if the thing itself had been awe struck by the sight.

"There must be a thousand buff down there," Chance would say. His thrill. Then he would take the car, like a sea captain gone bats, off the track and down into the valley, into that ocean of buffalo. A black typhoon of buffalo, stampeding in all directions. You smelled their nerves, the dung sweet below you, the rich warmth of their thighs. In them. Racing them. "They love it!" he would shout over the noise, the thunder of their anger and fear. "They love to move out!" Stretching his hand from the window, isolating a bull and reaching out as if to catch the animal, a hand that grazed the bull's flank, rode to the shoulder as the car gained and the beast failed, until Chance could grab a horn and wrench the great head around to show its terror-ridden eyes.

"Is it over?" To hear her tiny voice, to see her horrified, all part of the satisfaction. They would sit there for a few minutes while he smoked. Far into the curve of the valley the buffalo would calm and gather, a few still watching the strange machine. The rest would go back to eating while Chance and Christine watched, left there in the dust.

At the end of the day, looking at her sketches, Christine was stopped by one in which the tree had peculiarly human forms and these reminded her of Jim Chance. With a dark pen, she picked his gnarled torso from the pencil lines and shadows there, the sight of his body developing under her hand as if she were caressing him. She went to his tent and asked if he were awake, and when he said yes, she called him out with some story or other about wanting to take a walk since the moon was full, but she heard lions roaring, she said, and her sense of direction was off. The sounds had no origin, amplified by the high banks of the river, and she didn't want to walk right into them.

Any other man would have known what she wanted, but he was obtuse, or oblivious, so that she wondered what went on with him and Arlette beyond the *crêpes de banane flambées* that he ranted about, the reason he went to town at all. He said he would walk with her if she wanted, but instead they sat by the river and drank wine.

He talked, drowning her mood. She wished for silence. "I've killed a lot of elephant," he said, "and I don't mind admitting it. But at least I always had a license. And I always gave the meat to the *watu*. A license wasn't cheap either. You had to sell the tusks to a bloody Asian and he was the bastard who made the money. You were damn lucky if you had enough after it was over to buy another bloody goddamn license. Now there are no more licenses, no more hunters, that is, *legal* hunters. Well, it gives me a job, catching the bloody bastards. . ." There were pauses in his talk. In them the moon floated up into the sky and you could hear the heavy soft sounds of hippo coming out of the river to forage at night, like someone in the next bed rolling over, like a rustle of sheets. Christine couldn't understand what had been her desire for him in the first place except an image of something quick and uncomplicated, as detached as forms set in pencil and shaded on her pages. It occurred to her that this was what had gone wrong with the portraits, and she worried that she was going into a cold territory, rooted like the devil trees in hell.

"Okay, so why did I want to kill elephant? Because I was angry. And when you're angry, you want to kill things. I'm talking about when you're angry at God, if you believe in God, which I just happen to. So you come to a place like this and you kill, you wreck things, you defile because this is God's place. When you smash it, it's just like slapping God right across the face. Isn't there someone in the Bible like that? Well, if there isn't, put me in it."

She didn't know what he was talking about, a voice that beat against her own dark ideas despite the moon, isolated and brilliant, in the sky. All she wanted to think about were the hippo out there under the moon, whispering through the bush that surrounded the camp.

"Angry at God?" she asked. He was so important with it, and his rage.

He led her by the hand to a place just below where they sat, back away from the river, to the remains of a small shed. A circle of stones outside the door marked the place where someone had cooked. The tin roof was corroded and moonlight seeped in through it and through the broken mud walls. The shed had a hallowed look, like a shrine, as though it were being preserved. Inside there was a pallet still covered by an old sheet, and on a small table, a few pots and dishes, a chipped cup.

"I lived here," Jim Chance told her. He stood behind her, blocking the door.

"In here," she repeated.

"When I was a hermit," he said. "For six months I

never left the place. I ate nothing but the maize meal I carried in on my back. When I came out I started hunting. I killed elephant. I killed leopard. Buff. Kudu." He sat on the stone near the fireplace. "I was in mourning. There was this girl I was going to marry. She died of cancer. It took exactly six months for her to die. I made up for her suffering."

"That's why you were angry at God?"

"You'll never understand," he said. "No one will."

"Then why did you bring me here?" she asked him.

"Not to make you feel sorry for me. Just don't feel sorry for me."

"I won't then." She didn't. Instead she was surprised. Because she couldn't believe she was capable of the emotion that his gesture seemed to suggest. Love? She didn't believe he was capable of love; in fact, she didn't believe in love. Each person had a flaw which made love impossible outside imagination, tore into everything—how you lived, how you shared, what you gave, what you received, all the things people did when they weren't sitting around thinking about love. She had been raised as a Catholic and told about the perfect love of Jesus, an image of it, like blood, flowing from his wounds, or rays of light from heaven. It was all a little too made up, Jesus too flamboyant, too dramatic, with his love pouring out in miracles, almost as if it came from another source, onto a favored few. She wanted to believe, when she read biblical studies, the controversial theories about the Son of Man. One said the crucifixion was a plot, the Messiahhood simply acted out as it had been written, in staged events. Lazarus, the scholar wrote, was Christ's best friend. And in an article one Easter, a Jesuit admitted that Jesus couldn't have been the gentle, benign, sweet man of his own myth. Gentle, harmless men are not executed, the priest had written. There was the real Jesus and the image.

She began to think of mystical love as sexual: she had

marched as Christ's bride, taken his flesh between her lips. The rest was supplication, pleas for mercy, for favors, on your knees, as a beggar burdened with sin. It made no sense that this was love. It was merely living, acting out the same things that made up each day outside of worship—how you lived, how you shared, what you gave, what you received. Sitting each afternoon by your mother as the day stilled, the moment close, darkening toward the winter solstice or brightening in the spring, waiting each day for the moment when the man you both loved, your father, her husband, would come through the door. What will he be like today? Happy or raging, or silent, or tired. If you had only done all the things he wanted you to do, if you had only known, only guessed. Always ready to be sorry, to plead. Silent at the table over the food that he might not like, but at least not turning over the plates. Better the silence. Because you never knew what was inside him.

God's edict, "Judge ye not, lest ye be judged," made her laugh in a world that was full of crimes like His, but sometimes when her thoughts were the most bitter, the blackest, she would think of those words, knowing they were wise even if they did mock the humans they sought to counsel. You judged. You were judged. The way of the world despite all God's warnings, the One who did not make us perfect.

Judgment was why, after all, her portraits had been praised. "A merciless eye," one critic wrote and actually admired her for it. A few of her friends and subjects felt betrayed, even hurt, by some of the drawings. "Is that the way you see me?" as though she had no right. She told herself she had to be ruthless, the province of the artist. But when she had hepatitis she was so sick that she truly glimpsed mortality, or so she thought—her yellowed skin, her lost menstruation, the thick dark urine, the chalky stools—and she couldn't draw another human being after that.

She tried, she didn't know why, to make an illustration of Chance's story, perhaps as a way to let the truth about what he had told her overtake her senses. Her material was the man, the place, and this girl she had never seen, who had no portrait, no features, just the phantom outline. She used transparencies like double exposures in a photograph: images, the rivers of the Selous, the strange trees, the leopard with a claw raked through a skull, the faceless figure of a woman, the wild manner of his grief. She let the drawings spill freely without worrying what fell onto the page and afterward went through them the way she did, sometimes to look for what was simply pleasing to the sight, and sometimes like a person talking to herself to find the answers to her questions, or to answer the ones she had asked. One thing—the ghostlike outline of the girl worked best when it was superimposed on Chance, and in the most remarkable picture they merged so completely that he seemed to become the girl herself, her face his face. This was how Christine understood the meaning of his act—"I made up for her suffering."—living that way until he could put himself in her place, as if the time, space, even death, had ceased to matter.

At last she put her own features on the girl, self-portrait of a ghost, and then the three of them made a tangle, an endless knot. She played with the design until there was nothing but a circle, an abstraction, when she had always prided herself on realism, the merciless eye. Here everything to identify her characters had disappeared. She thought of a mandala without really knowing what one was. Her only image was of the tornado that had passed over their house one summer when she was a child, spent, a wide ring of clouds and wind. You saw a wheel in the sky as objects fell—a dress dropping absurdly to the lawn on a hanger with a price tag—things that began and ended outside of sense, somehow widening, giving themselves to the sky.

She asked Chance if she could do his portrait and he said, "Sure, why not?—another wild animal." He tried not to pose but he couldn't help it, braced in a camp chair with his head held at a certain angle. She discovered that she could draw him easily from life, though now, because she knew about him, he didn't look the same. She had been wrong to think she knew who he was.

"I'm really a portrait artist," she told him. "Not wild-life, that's something new." She relaxed behind the figure, somehow pleased. He took it to mean that she had finished and rose slowly, stiffly. "May I?" almost shy, he came around behind her to look. It was his head and torso and he looked very sad, very lonely and confused, not like the man he wanted to be. She expected him to hate the drawing—"Is that the way you see me?"—but instead he studied it for a long time and finally said, "I like that." He stayed behind her. "Is it finished? I don't know about stuff like that."

It was still morning. Mugo had gone down to the river for catfish so they walked along the bank until they saw him and called down. He looked up and waved them on. Chance ran, jumping down the bank ahead of her, but she didn't follow. She turned up into the grove of ancient trees, her quiet subjects with their hidden wells. There was no way to describe it—not even in the image of him she had just copied—how she had seen through, what she felt inside, this energy, not entirely her own.

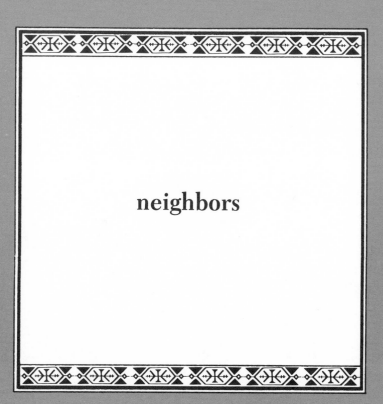

neighbors

Another white woman lived in the house before I did and everyone stared at her, too. "You get used to it," she told me. When I first moved in, kids shouted *mzungu* at me in case I didn't know I was different. They chased me to the bus stop begging for candy, a kind of extortion, but I held out and they gave up. The woman who lived here before had warned, "Watch out what you get started. Some things you can never get yourself out of." She was talking about water, not candy. She was talking about my bathtub, one of the few in the tiny tract of houses that had indoor plumbing. Everyone else had to get water from the tap at the corner, which, unfortunately, was dry a lot of the time. And so, from my predecessor, I inherited the responsibility of keeping this tub full at all times, a neighborhood reservoir.

One day, desperate for a bath, I forgot the tap was dry and plunged in, sank into the cool water there with the same sigh I might have used back in Vermont on a December night, where the water would have been hot but no less welcoming. There was that same reassuring lap, water licking porcelain like lake kissing shore. It gave me a lost feeling, dense with nostalgia. Out my window where the sun did what no northern sun could do, banana leaves were layered in succulent greens and the pervasive smell of grated coconut charmed the air. I lathered up and sang.

It was the sight of my feet that suddenly accused me of polluting the neighborhood water supply. By the time I reached them with the soap, small eddies of mud and other things were loosening. Just the ring around my tub was enough to make me certain that even in the garden this stuff would be considered toxic waste. At that guilty moment, however, I got a brilliant idea of installing some kind of water tank out by tap number 7, a community self-help project. Though I am a linguist, a lexicographer brought out to build quick vocabularies in places where language and technology were out of kilter, everyone assumed I was a Peace Corps volunteer. My neighbors often brought me things to fix or came looking for medicine. They expected me to supply them with seeds at planting time. One of them thought that I had come to teach them all how to screen their windows. But I never did anything like that and wondered if they suspected my presence had some nefarious purpose beyond the learning of their language. If it hadn't been for the water in my tub, I probably wouldn't have known anyone.

Sophia Mturi, who lived directly behind me, listened carefully to my idea. "We can all work together and build"—here, speaking Swahili, I had to use an elaborate construction—"a very large bucket in which to put water laid by for the future."

"Ooo," she said, "*tenki*."

"Yes, *tenki*," I replied. Like a badgered member of the Académie Française, these rank Englishisms haunted me. Tenki. Benki. Motaa caah.

Sophia, a sanophile with no spigot, had six kids and a husband, Palangyo, to wash clothes for. She washed everything, in fact, and was known to visit my cistern many times on dry days. Palangyo worked as a cook in a European house and whenever they had cocktail parties, Palangyo emptied all the glasses. Though he insisted his employers were Spanish, Sophia believed they were French because they didn't get around to eating supper until past ten o'clock, and once it got that late, Palangyo didn't bother to come home. Americans, she said, were the best people to work for because they ate at six o'clock, paid the most, and had machines to wash and dry the clothes, machines that their servants could always sneak in to use. Sadly, Americans always fired Palangyo because the memsaabs couldn't stand his drinking. Sophia figured that her father had benefited most from her marriage—twelve cows, since she was literate and also, by her own admission, beautiful, big and plump with the fine, creamy skin attributed to people who ate plaintain three times a day.

She like the idea of this water tank, but was wary. "Who will keep tricky people from taking too much and leaving nothing?" she said, though she was the most likely to offend.

I said I thought that in the spirit of self-help and cooperation, if everyone worked together, no one would steal since stealing only meant stealing from yourself.

She looked. "I can see you don't know Africans," she said.

We made a list anyway, of what to do and how to proceed, and the sight of the writing, some of it her own, fired her imagination. We needed a plan, she said. *Mpango.* From *kupanga*, putting everything in order. She wrote: one, two, three. We needed to find out how much it would cost. We needed to get official permission. Finally, we had to get the money. It even fired my imagination, for I had been thinking more in terms of a few steel drums and a length of hose. When there was water at the tap, you filled the drums; when there wasn't you used what was in them. Sort of like my tub. Suddenly I did feel like a Peace Corps volunteer.

The other neighbors, ones who used tap number 7, were interested enough to agree to attend a meeting.

Helen and Norbert Manda, who lived on my left, were generally keen on improvements. They had put little wooden shutters on their windows, for example, and kept potted plants in tins on their front porch. It was usually on weekends that Helen came shyly and politely to my door with her small kettle. Then in order to compensate for the inconvenience, she had me to tea. They both worked in "offices" it was said and had enough money to acquire lots of things, most of them second-hand and broken on purchase. They lived in constant search of spare parts and repair men.

Paul Ntila, who lived on my right and called me "Sistah" or "Missus," depending on the view of Americans held forth in the daily news, kept his water stored in plastic jugs and when those ran out, went to stay with friends. But he was committed. "Because of the others suffering," he said, "I will join."

Sophia told me that instead of a wife, Ntila had a radio-cassette, reasoning that since the cost of this machine certainly equaled the price of a bride, he had chosen the one over the other. We sat at my table with sheets of lined paper making lists and checking names. Sophia could only write by leaning over with her head at the edge of the table looking up toward her hand because, she said, she had learned it that way, a tiny girl at a very big desk. Mr. Ntila, she said, worked at the Ministry of Works, which made him rich, though he bought nothing but cassettes to play in his machine and late into the night. The music kept Sophia awake, wondering where Palangyo was, night after night. To that end, she had scrimped and saved and finally got her husband a used bicycle so he could speed back and forth and come home regularly.

Sophia had drafted the neighbors who lived on either side of her. The papers that she carried around and worked on and the adherence of the Mponji household, consisting of elders, gave weight to the project, an air of legitimacy. Baba Mponji had two wives, one old and one young, and he rented the living room of his house to Baba Abdullah, a mullah, and his old and only wife, Mariam. On the other side was Candida Rweyemamu, who had her husband's extended family living over there and who needed as much water as she could get. They had built ramshackle additions to the house to fit everyone in. Two of her husband's nephews lived in a cardboard box covered with plastic out behind the kitchen.

Everyone attended our first meeting at tap number 7. Though it was a stinking hot night, there was a Northern Hemisphere energy, a fit of cooperation, chaired by Sophia, who frequently jotted on her pad or pretended to, since I knew her upright angle made it impossible. She selected Ntila and me to determine the costs, which she called the "billings" in English, though God knows where she got the word. Perhaps from an Indian. Helen and Norbert Manda, who were to get the official permission, served us all tea. Then, in the middle of a long speech about hope and the future that Baba Mponji was delivering, Palangyo appeared and our meeting collapsed. He announced that he had been badly beaten and robbed of his bicycle. He'd been coming home late the night before when thieves jumped out of the bushes. He had to spend most of the day at the police station.

Sophia ran to him. A voice rose, Baba Abdullah's, complaining of the times and the fall of man. Kids, excited by the upset, raced, pulling on each other's clothes. Words were lost to me then; I could only sense them falling like rain around me. Helen Manda had stayed back and was looking at me and I could tell she was so embarrassed. She had a long, gentle face. Her hair was plaited in a simple style, her dress remarkably fresh and clean, a nun's aura, sad and neat, with clasped hands.

On our pricing trip, Paul Ntila talked about Palangyo's bicycle, abandoned in a village near the bay, found and then returned to him by the police—two improbable events. The bicycle had been damaged, yes, but *found*. And *returned*.

"In fact," I said, "this morning when he got on it, the chain fell off." A crisis, in which Baba Mponji, known as a mechanic, and three of the Candida in-laws worked for an hour to get the thing back together and running. Ntila, who was wearing a cravat and sunglasses, said something about simple people and simple machines, but his English wasn't good enough to make the thought clear.

We took a sketch of the water tank to a welder down in the market. Chickens picked among the stacks of charcoal braziers and recycled tin cans made into kerosene lamps. I loved these places where people made the things they sold, where it seemed you could order anything. Elementary in all the good connotations of that word; you knew where what you got came from. I would miss this when I went home, where manufacture meant something else. Ntila was talking to the welder who leaned, as if exhausted, against a pile of bedsprings. We also consulted a carpenter since the tank was to be raised on legs so that the women could easily draw the water into their buckets from a tap at the bottom. In the end, we figured we needed a total of five hundred shillings, which, divided by each household, would be about eighty-five shillings or, by adult person, as Ntila suggested, about thirty-five shillings: the cost, he said, of two cassettes. He frowned. "I will have to pay a bride price soon," he confided.

That night near the tap we presented our results. Helen and Norbert Manda thought it fairer to pay by adult person, but everyone else looked glum because even twenty shillings seemed too much.

"As for myself," Candida said, "I use all my money. If I save some aside I will only use it."

"This is why we are poor," Sophia complained.

Candida's sister-in-law suggested time payments, "We will slowly-slowly give our money to Baba Abdullah. Of all the men, he is most honest." The baba held his hands in a grateful manner and touched his heart.

"When the time comes," Sophia told me after the group had separated, "and you count this slowly-slowly saving, you will only have to know how to count to zero."

I thought about it a minute and said, "What if I charged money for the water in my tub? Until each person paid? It could be a way to save," which on the surface sounded like a great idea.

"But the ones who are short of money, how will they pay, and how will you tell them no?" She used the term *shati-mahney.* Now, I love languages the way some people love vintage wine or gourmet food, but I could never turn in anything like *"shati-mahney"* to my fellow professionals with their computerized word hunts: they were purists and *shati-mahney* was plonk. What you guzzled when you wanted to get drunk.

When Sophia saw some of the others a few days later at the kiosk, they reached a consensus that paying for the water in my tub was a good method of raising funds and decided informally that I could simply hand over what I collected to Baba Abdullah for safekeeping. I was to hand out credit and debit chits to keep the record. *Cheti,* as they were called after the colonial fixation.

Norbert and Helen Manda were good for it right away and paid the whole balance on the first tea kettle. Even Ntila appeared, flush, saying he had sold some of his cassettes and a pair of old shoes to raise money. He winked because I knew why. He had a sense of duty, wanted to be a good neighbor, he said, and took a saucepan of water to boil his rice.

He asked me, "Are you a Peace Corps?" What he said was Peace Corpse.

"No," I told him, "I work at the Swahili Institute;

they're looking for new words to keep up with the modern world."

"You?" He looked puzzled. I wondered if it was the idea of me or the idea of the project. "But you don't speak very well. A little, but not *very.*"

"In fact," I said, "you don't need to speak at all." This would have been hard to explain. It amused him though. He shrugged and left. We had stepped out of my door in the last of the afternoon. Flies were hanging in the shade of banana leaves, too hot and tired to buzz, and the dust had puffed, fine as powder, to form a cloud around us. The whole atmosphere made me happy.

Very early next morning, I was awakened by loud voices out back. Palangyo, who had fallen from his bicycle, was wailing that he had a broken leg. He told the story that he had mounted the bicycle to go to work when the seat fell off and the tires went flat, which dropped him to the ground. By the time I got out there, Sophia and the kids were all around poking at the fallen thing as if it could be prodded back to life. One of the Candida nephews appeared with a wrench, and Baba Mponji was fetched out of bed to fix it again. Palangyo's uniform, of course, was filthy, and the whole affair threw Sophia's compulsive wash schedule off. She came looking for water in my tub, chattering about how she thought the whole business with the bicycle was odd. Suspicious. There were plenty of words in her language for this. "How can a seat fall off, a chain fall off, tires go flat?" she asked.

I thought, somehow, she already had the answer in mind. "Bad things happen in threes," I told her lightly. "This is what we say in English. A proverb. The chain, the seat, the tire. This will be the end now.

It wasn't the end. The following day when Palangyo started out to work, he noticed the handlebars felt warm to his touch. They grew hotter and hotter as he went along and then, before he had gone very far at all, the bicycle started to shake violently and threw him off. Sophia's three eldest children and two of Candida's ran out and brought it back. By this time, Sophia was convinced that someone had put witchcraft on the bicycle, and although it was not a very modern thing to do, against her religion and the law, she went straight to a witch doctor.

Candida, dipping water on account, told me that, according to the witch doctor, the bicycle had been stolen that first night not by humans but by fiends, agents of a powerful witch who was living in our midst. "Someone paid this witch," she explained, "someone who is jealous of Palangyo and wants him to lose his job."

"What will you do about this?" I asked her.

"First, Sophia has to find out the witch," she said.

To do this, Sophia had been given a pot of a certain dark, oily, foul-smelling substance which she was instructed to paint on every door in the neighborhood, a small dot of it. Whenever a person who knew the identity of the witch passed through one of the doors, he or she would immediately fall down and be temporarily paralyzed. At this point he or she could be grabbed and made to reveal the identity of the witch. Candida had seen with her own eyes (she pointed) this very method work in the case of a thief who had stolen her towels. He fell down and could not move until he revealed where the towels had been hidden.

Sophia got busy painting dots. She even painted one on my door, which I went in and out of several times to prove my innocence. She sneaked a dot onto Ntila's door while he was away visiting his mother in Bagamoyo. Helen and Norbert Manda, however, refused to allow her to touch their door. I heard them arguing in loud, dry voices, using Swahili I didn't understand but that I got the gist of. Not only was witchcraft against the law, Norbert shouted, but Sophia was a stupid, ignorant fool to believe such things. I heard him tell her to go back to the bush, that it wasn't witchcraft, it was simply Palangyo having the d.t.'s. From my window, I saw Sophia run from them, her cream complexion deepened with fury like hand-dipped chocolate from the vat.

Sophia was convinced by this that Norbert and Helen had something to do with the curse on Palangyo's bicycle. Their refusal to have the medicine painted on their door was an announcement of guilt. She went from house to house like a vigilante. She even suggested that Helen herself was the witch. Why didn't Helen have any children? How did Helen have so much money, so many things? Candida said that one night she had seen a creature fly to the roof of Helen's house carrying something heavy and dark like the body of a child. One of her nieces corroborated the story, saying that the creature had a red comb like a rooster and smelled very bad. And so it went in the hot afternoons, sometimes around my tub, while Palangyo stayed home and skipped work. Who knew what story they were telling his employers, Spanish or French?

It was Paul Ntila who had the singular bad luck to trip and fall in his doorway on the afternoon he returned from his mother's while several of the Candida minions were standing by to see. Though he was not paralyzed on the spot, the event reverberated through the neighborhood and the man was grabbed. I listened from my window. Sophia ordered him to name the witch. Ntila didn't know any witch, he said. He didn't know anything about the queered bicycle. During all this, someone from another block rushed into his house, snatched his radio-cassette and threatened to smash it if he didn't talk. Was it like this in Salem, I wondered?

Baba Abdullah arrived, dressed in his mullah's outfit, and cried, "Stop this, please! Please! Please!" His arms were raised.

Norbert Manda, who passed on his way home from

work, shouted, "I will call the police! You will all go to jail!"

"He's protecting his wife! Let the girl tell us what she saw, what flew over this man's house." But the girl was running away and Norbert stormed off, swinging his briefcase like an angry executive.

I heard a voice then, perhaps Abdullah's, repeating, "Please, you must not throw stones!"

"If you throw stones," I called out to them, "then I'm going to get the police." I ran outside.

"Get them!" Ntila shouted. "That one over there has stolen my radio-cassette."

Baba Abdullah had reached my side; he touched my wrist. "I am embarrassed and ashamed," he whispered. "You must think of us as ignorant and foolish children." He warned the crowd, "God forbids this!"

One of the Candida nephews, a small one who lived in the box, asked me, "Have you witches in America?"

"You are a nincompoop," the baba told him, in English.

There was a lull. No one seemed to know what to do next. Except Ntila, who made a quick break and ran. In an instant he was gone. All the little gardens in our neighborhood had been planted to corn which was tall enough now for a man to slip and dart through, into the old banana plantation, down to the river and away, the route of thieves. The crowd scattered as if to give chase, but in fact, except for Sophia, who had a real stake in the palaver, no one else was interested enough to bother getting scratched up down there.

Helen's long face hung in the evening shade, a darker patch in the shadow of her porch. "You must wonder at us." She spoke as I came closer. "We are such terrible and stupid people." She spoke English beautifully.

"Actually, it's the bicycle I wonder about," I said.

"Yes, it is strange. Perhaps Palangyo has made it all up. You don't understand our people. He could easily make it all up," she said.

"But why?"

"Because of jealousy."

"Jealousy?" A word I had been hearing. *Wivu.* Stronger in Swahili for its two syllables.

"Yes," she sighed. "So his enemies would be blamed."

Draped by a blanket of children, Abdullah was still guarding Ntila's door when the police arrived, followed by Ntila in a taxi.

"This is a terrible foolishness," Abdullah said, "Forgive us." He opened his palms.

Ntila was angry, scowling, looking around. The police took names, but it was really the radio-cassette Ntila wanted—his tapes and a few other valuables. In the end, he stood in front of the baba and said, "I want my money, the money from the water tank, thirty-five shillings." He looked accusingly at me, as if I had a part in all this.

"And mine as well!" Norbert Manda said from behind. "*Yangu pia!*"—so that he could explode that *p* like an invective.

"No, no . . ." Helen was saying. She was all eyes ringed black and a hairdo of sprung twists. Her hands were clasped like prayer.

But the baba had opened his pouch and was emptying the water-tank account. A few shillings remained, clinking sadly.

"We have fallen low," he said. In his robe he gleamed like a white column. A black prayer mark on his forehead glowered at the crowd.

We were left suddenly with the quiet night. I squished a trail of ants noiselessly following the path between our houses. Ntila's was all locked up now, unlighted, a gloomy thing.

"He'll move away," Sophia said. "Now we can never find out the witch."

A breeze. A smell of blooming, maybe jasmine, a

reminder of sweet times. I thought of my tub in there, full of cool water. The taps were running and the bath was mine. I could soak the night away, just a little melancholy with the thought of that drained purse.

"But you don't *really* believe in witches, do you?" I asked Sophia.

"What do you know?" she said. She walked away, past the bicycle, chained there to the tree and worthless, like stock in a bankrupt company. She tugged listlessly at the bewitched handlebars.

The witch doctor said the only thing they could do now was to destroy the bicycle itself. Baba Mponji and crew did this according to a detailed set of instructions, wrenching and pounding, as Palangyo looked miserably from his window. Sophia's job, once the fiendish machine was dismantled, was to deposit the various bits of rubber and metal here and there in very secret locations. She also had anointed sticks, which she was supposed to bury six steps from each of the four corners of her house. But even so, the curse could not be foiled and Palangyo did lose his job, though some of us thought it was because he had been absent so much.

"Any curse will come so if you make it," Norbert Manda said.

And Helen said, "Mr. Ntila has moved away. He came in a pickup and collected all his things." She seemed sadder than usual, which purified her even more.

A couple with a baby arrived to rent Ntila's old house, and because they need gallons of water to wash diapers, the idea of selling the contents of my tub to raise money for the storage tank was revived. We gathered once again on a cloudy evening near tap number 7, which had been dry for three days. Even my tub was empty. Baba Abdullah made a long speech about everyone sharing troubles. I could only understand a little and the proverb that I knew: "The rain does not fall on one roof alone." I was reintroduced to the group as a Peace Corps volunteer. There was a good feeling again. We sat on wooden chairs and drank a pot of millet beer that Mama Mponji had brewed.

Palangyo's bicycle was still with us. Kids in the neighborhood were claiming that at night they had seen it, a phantom, going along with no one on it.

"I saw a *shetani* riding it," one of the Candida nephews said. A chameleon *shetani* (Did I know the one?) familiar to everyone by its popping eyes and long, furious tongue.

"You cannot see *shetani*," Candida said. "If you look on a *shetani*, you will drop dead instantly."

"Then what did I see?"

There were a few drops of rain then, though no one bothered to move. It felt too good.

"Rain," I said, perhaps stupidly.

"Yes," Baba Abdullah agreed.

"Good," Sophia said.

And then, as more came, people started to move along, to get their basins out to catch what they could. In the morning, as I went to look for new words in my computer, I'd see them all out, washing cloths in the puddles that gathered in the hard, baked earth.

abdullah
and
mariam

Baba Abdullah had been giving me Swahili lessons three afternoons a week for almost a year. Though we were neighbors and the atmosphere casual, he dressed for the occasion. His brown, double-breasted, gabardine suit shone with age, but it had been carefully saved, used only with a purpose: it wasn't threadbare; it had never been mended. On his necktie was a picture of Queen Elizabeth. On his head, the finely embroidered skullcap of Islam. On his forehead, the black prayer mark of a holy man. During Ramadan, he wore a white suit, lapels so wide they reached to his shoulders. In the holy season our classes drifted to sleep with his fatigue. He was too old to fast, he admitted, but he did it anyway—to atone, he claimed, for Ramadans long ago when he had fallen astray.

"I will tell you this, Mamma," he said, "there were many Ramadans when I did not observe the fast. I was, well, a dissolute young man with many coins in my pockets." He grinned as if he didn't believe it either. "I dressed with a hat, thus. A cravat, like the English. And *cigarettes*! I smoked, Mamma, oh, yes, I did smoke." He tipped his head.

The past hung on Baba Abdullah like his old, ill-fitting suits. There were his regrets. He had been selected by the British to attend a university in London, a very great honor, but he chose not to go. His father was old, he said, his mother ailing. It seemed so far away from Africa, and he was a Moslem. They wouldn't understand his religion, his kind. He had heard of the terrible coldness there, of the ice and snow and endless rain. He always missed the education, although he discovered that everything he, a simple man, ever needed was in the Koran. Perhaps, he acknowledged, such a life would not be enough for an American like me, and yes, there was a time when he had listened to Bach and Mozart and felt his soul lift. But that was long ago.

"When you go home to your cold place," he told me, "and you are as old as I am, you will remember the sweet taste of our mangoes in just this way."

He regretted his marriage. He should have remained celibate, he said. Not that he didn't love his wife, but, by Allah's will and his mysterious work, Abdullah had been stricken barren, and his poor wife had suffered the pain of the childless woman in Africa. They had adopted two abandoned children, a boy and a girl. Abdullah never spoke about the girl, but the boy was bad. They had never been able to stop him from stealing. Now he was in jail.

"I am so very sorry, Mamma," he said, apologizing as though he had offended me, had let me down in some way. I had never seen Abdullah's wife. I knew she was old, infirm. And I knew she was cherished. Sophia saved things for her from the shopping—"Binti Mariam likes these mangoes from Tabora. . . . These nice tomatoes are for Binti Mariam. . . ." Candida Mpongi crocheted things for the binti, and Helen Mutasingwa called on the old woman at least once a week.

One day Baba Abdullah was beaten and robbed by young hoodlums downtown. Sophia told me, "They knocked the baba down. They took his money. They tore up his clothes. Nothing is as it was. The whole world has been spoiled." The double-breasted suit was beyond repair. "*Watu gani*?" she asked. "What kind of people are these?"

It was easy enough for Sophia and Candida to collect money around the neighborhood and buy him another suit, used, but in good condition. They were pleased with their purchase, a more up-to-date number, single breasted, pin-striped, three-piece. They brought it to him in the hospital and he wore it home. The trousers were wide, gathered by his old belt, puckering around his waist, the jacket was over his arm, and the vest, like an awning, covered his thin frame. Binti Mariam walked near him on Sophia's arm, bent with arthritis and covered by the black cape and hood of a traditional Swahili woman.

I greeted them as they passed. The baba asked me for my news and I asked for his. His news was good, he said, but not so good. The wounds on his body had healed; those in his heart had not. Binti Mariam smiled my way. She still had a beautiful face.

When Baba Abdullah came the following week to give me a language lesson, he was wearing his white suit. It was not Ramadan. I thought he must have been having the pin-stripe altered, and, as we were exchanging news in greeting, I asked him about the new suit, complimenting Sophia and Candida on their choice.

"Oh, Mamma, I'm so sorry," he said sadly. "I'm afraid I have sold it." His wife needed surgery, he said; her gall bladder. He had taken her to a private hospital, the hospital used by the expatriates where there were the very best doctors. It was so expensive he didn't think the suit would be enough to pay for it all.

He told me, "Yes-yes, those ruffians were not the first to beat me. Please, let me tell you a story. When I was a young man, Mamma, I was an interpreter for the British. On one occasion they sent me to Lake Tanganyika to help supervise the shipment of goods to the Belgian Congo. (Now that country is called Zaire; nothing is as it was.)"

"I remember those days well. I dressed in a new suit, directly from England. You could order things then from catalogues, if you can believe it. In those days, I'm sorry to tell you, I took cigarettes, yes, and I even drank whiskey. I had a very fine hat, all the fashion, with a wide brim. I remember it was a hat of dark brown and I bought it from a white man who later became my friend. His name was Dr. Leichester. He knew Swahili, Mamma! How he loved Swahili. Together we translated many poems. And we wrote a grammar; someday I will show you. A fine man. He sold me his hat at a very good price and when I went away to serve the king at the lake, he gave me a feather to put in the band like an Englishman. We were young, you see, and very foolish. Oh, how I dressed in those days. I went about so." Abdullah squared his shoulders and swayed from side to side.

"I spent each day at the lake. I carried a big ledger and many pens. I was such a young man and I thought these things were important. Then we watched shipments of all sorts in and out of the Congo where the Belgians lived. My goodness, I even learned a little French!" He laughed at himself.

He went on: "In Tanganyika, as the country was known in those days, not Tanzania as we are now—we have changed, Mamma, we have changed!—there were many Germans. I'm very sorry to say this but they were cruel men. Not like the English. They had a terrible whip like a millet stalk with five fingers of leather to sting the skin of a man. I'm ashamed to admit, but despite these wicked things, I fancied myself a white man. It was very wrong of me.

"One day I made a journey across the lake and into the Congo, and there I learned that the Belgians were even more cruel than the Germans. So help me, they were truly coarse men. I saw them working, bent like black men to their tasks, and I thought perhaps they were prisoners. But no! My friends and I laughed at this, fools, not thinking that white men could do this kind of work. Oh, their backs were very sore from the sun, and red, but their bodies were strong. My, yes.

"There were other men there, in uniforms, walking along the quays, shouting and whipping the Africans. So much commotion and so much blood. I had never seen anything like this and I was frightened. My suit and my ledgers, my pens and my fine English hat with the feather could not change what I knew I was—a hated man. I see I am making you unhappy with this." I shook my head, and though he seemed to want to end the tale, he went on.

"Right in front of my feet a Belgian officer began to beat a black boy, no more than fifteen years, a young boy. I stepped between them and stayed the white man's hand. He lifted back on his toes to strike me and, so help me, Mamma, I pushed him down! As he stumbled to rise, I'm afraid, in my anger, I kicked his head. I wore English riding boots, even in the hot weather. It was my heel that struck his temple." The old baba gave me a shy, hesitant grin, the grin of a holy man. "He was very, *very* angry. Then all too fast it happened: I pushed him into the water, thus. . ." Abdullah rose from his chair, his arms out and his hands scooping the air. "Of course, by then, the others had grabbed me. It was easy for them. I swear I did not know how to fight, you see. Even so, I felt a strange joy. I have never felt it again. Does it shock you? The Belgian came from the water and hit me, but I could feel nothing against my joy. He ripped my clothes and I didn't care. He pulled my splendid hat and threw it in the water. I watched it, Mamma, float away, the feather so gay. And then my heart began to ache. We are truly fallen creatures.

"They took me to jail. I'm afraid I must not tell you how it was there: it would hurt you too much to know of these things, but there was a joke to it, don't you see. I, in my fine suit, my leather boots from England, my cigarettes, my cravat—so I began to laugh. When Allah gives to you the strength to laugh, then Mamma, you will survive all things. They beat me many times, many times. I nearly died. I had a terrible fever. It is my belief this fever caused me to become barren.

"I wasn't married then, of course, but I wish to tell you the parents of Binti Mariam and my own parents had arranged for our union in the old-fashioned way. Even so, we were making a love marriage: we had selected each other, you see, and then pressed our parents to agree. In those days, Mamma, it was a very daring thing to do. Perhaps you think I am an old fool. Yes, yes,"—he smiled—"there was a deep love between us, even then. I sent her a letter that I was in prison. She received it months later. She still has the letter, I promise you.

"Now, as you know, Mamma, the prisons here do not supply food or medicine or clothes. Not even water. We were thrown about like trash." He chuckled. "It remains for our wives and mothers to keep us alive when we are prisoners. They bring us our food and the things we need. Since I had no wife or mother there in the Congo, I had to take food from my fellows, a hard thing for me to do, who had been so foolish and proud.

"Well, my goodness! That girl, Mariam, ran away from Dar es Salaam. Can you imagine? In *those* days? Of course, now it is a common thing: the young are running here and there. But listen to how she did it. She dressed herself as a ragged little boy and came all the way into the Congo, a terrible long journey. She found me. She did it without help. When she came to me she was still dressed as a boy child. Her hair was cut, her knees poking from torn pants, but excuse me for saying it, her eyes were— well, I can't tell you, oh, no, that would spoil it for me! She found work soon there in the house of a Belgian family. A maid, she cared for their children. She, from that fine family: her father, I assure you, owned many houses on Zanzibar. For two years, Mamma, she came to the prison with my food, with the medicines for me when I was sick, with clean clothes when mine were dirty. And she was the one who cured the hatred in my heart. With such hatred, I could not have lived on. I think you understand. Sadly, her family did not welcome us back after this. She had run away, you see. Nothing could ever make up for that shame. She was utterly lost. Yes, they were too harsh in those days, too harsh. Well, since then, we have been alone. There has been sadness, but Allah has blessed us in other ways." It was his way of explaining, I could see, that they had precious debts to each other. They were different from other people, at least he thought so, and I suppose she did, too.

We were quiet. I fixed him tea. Then we translated a poem. It made us laugh the way it seemed to spring, as if it had known what we were talking about, from the anthology, *A Choice of Flowers* — what the Swahili call their poetry. I took it line by line as he pondered, knowing translation would never suffice.

"*Wameshindwa watu kweli,*" I began. "'These are the ones who are truly defeated.' *Wazazi wa majumbani*: 'parents in their houses,'" I said. Well, *majumbani*; not houses exactly, something bigger, a place, perhaps a state of mind, their ways. "'Parents fixed in their ways,'" I corrected.

"Yes, that is good, Mamma. You have the feel for it. 'Fixed in their ways' is better than 'houses,'" he said.

"*Wenye kutowa ukali—,*" I tried the whole poem from there, "'Ones who show harshness with pleasure on their lips. They will be people distant from us. What can anyone do? Because when we are together, we are—'" Here, I stopped. The word was *peponi*. It meant paradise, heaven. But it also means in the wind. "'We are in the wind'? 'Part of the wind'? 'We are the wind'?" I asked.

He was smiling, seeing how I wanted to play with the

word, hands folded on his chest. "*Tuko peponi.* 'We are in heaven,' Mamma. But yes, 'we are part of the wind', invisible. This is nice. 'When we are together, we are part of wind.' You must ask, then, what things will hold us still, hold us to earth. If you are part of the wind, you will be carried, sometimes gently but sometimes with danger, as in a storm. This, of course, is the beauty of poetry. So many meanings, in words so simple."

"'Because when we are together,'" I said again, "'We are aloft' (I was inspired), 'we are currents on the wind.'" And he was nodding, swaying, his eyes closed as if he were that free.

He was the one who whispered the rest in English, "'We will ignore them all. Why do they wonder really? Surely we are not the first. People began this long ago. Yes, long ago. People and this kind of love. Isn't that so?'" It was a wonderful lesson. The baba still wore a bandage over one eyebrow from his ordeal and he limped a little from a bruise on his leg as he stepped out of my house and walked away.

Sophia, of course, was glum when she realized that Baba Abdullah had sold the suit. But, knowing why, she couldn't say anything to him about it. She got over it soon and there were preparations concerning the binti's return from the hospital. I asked her if she knew the story of Abdullah and Mariam. It seemed a great love story to me, one they all must know. She nodded and told me, "Yes, and for two years, Binti Mariam took food to him. She went to that faraway place dressed as a boy. Against her parents. She became so thin and hungry that her monthly blood stopped and never returned. With no monthly blood there could be no children. But the baba never took a second wife and so he has no sons."

"Did the binti tell you this?" I asked her. I was thinking of what he had always said about his barrenness. Not hers.

"Everyone knows," she answered. "They are good people. Very good. Not like the rest of us."

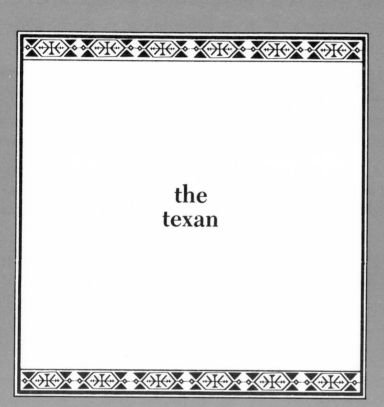

the
texan

The consular officer had a good time telling everyone about how he got the Texan out of jail. It was the littlest Texan the consular officer ever saw and after five days in the gerzie (that is to say the *gereza*, the clinker, the hoosegow, or whatever you call it) he was, without doubt the *meanest* Texan anyone ever wanted to see. He had the string pulled in around those prison pj's so tight his Lone Star eyes were popping. Wouldn't touch the gerzie food, so he was just about starved. This cowpoke looked like his blood was nourishing on bile. Had gone bottle green, like a lizard, and was hopping mad. The consular officer was afraid that, given time, the Texan would kill him another African. Yes, he would.

The Texan didn't carry a diplomatic passport and had no real immunity, but he did work for the American government, and the consular officer claimed that, in theory, under what they call a bilateral agreement, the buckaroo was, in fact, immune and could not be tried under foreign laws. That was the theory. This was Africa. Therefore, since the ambassador his-very-self had ordered that someone get the Texan o-u-t of the country f-a-s-t, the consular officer resorted to extralegal methods. Well, call them paralegal methods. Better yet, call them traditional methods. He bribed someone at the newspaper to put a lid on the story and then he got the dead man's family to agree to blood money. Five thousand bucks in shillings served in a plain manila envelope. After all, the man was dead and the Texan worth nothing to anybody locked up. So in one blazing moment of confusion, the dead man's folks declared the police had the wrong man and the consular officer slipped the scrawny American right into the Flying Doctor's plane and the hell out. Five grand was nothing at all: the Texan coughed it up without a whimper or a sigh. Look, they feed you typhoid soup and cholera sandwiches in the gerzie. Maybe, the consular officer added, the Texan could deduct the five biggies from his income tax.

The Texan felt a real downhome zeal when he took the job in Africa. He felt like a combination Connecticut Yankee in King Arthur's court and Albert Schweitzer. Customs officials found the contents of his luggage strange: a few pounds of aspirin, a case of Band-Aids, all kinds of hand mirrors, tiny flashlights, boxes of zippers, toy scissors, needles, threads, tubes of glue, metal belt buckles, you name it. One of the bureaucrats that came out and hired the Texan had told him, "Look, they haven't discovered the wheel yet over there. Some of 'em haven't started using fire. Henh-henh-henh."

So imagine the Texan's surprise when he was met at the plane in Nairobi, Kenya, and taken in a big white Chevy along a divided highway, past a drive-in movie, to the tenth floor of a Hilton where he was served a cheeseburger and two cold beers. Only difference between this room and El Paso, the Texan reflected, was that everyone was black. But that didn't bother him. Despite what everyone said about Southerners and their racial views, the Texan lived by one rule: any man shows me he's at least as good a man as I am, that's all I ask. He'd had black students and Indians come through his classes; some flunked, some got A's, just like anybody else. But vet science was no easy course and the black kids that stuck it out were few. The Texan knew it was because of some unfair start they were getting, the *big* unfair start they got a couple of hundred years ago, and maybe even before that when the Arabs and Europeans came down and wrecked their chances on the Dark Continent, too. The Texan's father went around El Paso telling everyone, "My son's going over to help the poor niggers out there in Africa."

A few days later, the same driver in the same Chevy took the Texan due south across the border into Tanzania to a town called Arusha. In the living room of some Americans who welcomed him with drinks and dinner, the Texan told a joke about how the Africans got this big old Holstein bull from America to breed with and upgrade their local stock. Weeks went by. After about six, seven months, the Africans ask if something is bothering the bull. Food, change of water, change of weather? Too hot? Nope, the weather's fine, the bull says. Doesn't he like their gals? Bull says the gals are fine too, lovely ladies. What's the problem then? the Africans ask. Big Holstein says, "Hey, wait a minute, I was brought here to *advise*." The Americans laughed as though they never heard the joke before and the Texan told them how he wasn't going to be that kind of adviser. He came to Africa to practice animal medicine and to show some folks how it's done. The Americans wished him luck.

Now, the vet who had the job before the Texan had let everything the Americans started there fall apart. The vaccination campaigns were dead. All that remained were some old posters in places like grocery stores advertising the dangers of rinderpest. The dips the Americans had built to dredge cattle for parasites had long gone dry—cement tubs full of weeds now. The artificial-insemination centers were all but closed; only the employees remained, sitting at desks and drawing salaries. The freezers for the bull semen, American imports, had never worked well in the tropics and, once they had broken, there was no one to repair them. Out of five freezers, only one still worked. The Texan found it full of beer. When he reported the two men who were selling cold beer out of it, he was told they could not be fired.

The Texan inherited other problems from his predecessor—a cook, a gardener, and a night watchman. The cook bothered the Texan; he was slow, stretched out the pitiful chores to fill time by moving at quarter speed. And he was like a kid; he whined that he didn't have a bed, got the Texan to buy him one. Wanted the Texan to give him bus money to go visit his wife on weekends, wanted the Texan to give him a monthly allowance for sugar and milk. The Texan offered the man a higher salary if he would stop asking for extras. The cook took it, but the demands went on. He wanted tablets for his headaches, razor blades from the United States (the local ones made his face numb), soap for baths, and permission to use the Texan's hot shower on Saturday afternoon before he went on leave. And the cook made lousy food. On Mondays he cooked for the whole week, so everything tasted like leftovers. He went through quantities of tin foil. The refrigerator looked like a silver mine. But he was honest: all the Americans told the Texan that honest servants were hard to come by. And the cook never showed up drunk—another plus. They told the Texan to keep the guy.

The gardener was even more of a joke. In order to keep his work at a bare minimum, he cut down everything in the yard and burned it. When the Texan put in a vegetable garden, the gardener forgot to water it and all the seedlings died. The Texan joked with Americans who came to dinner, said he came from El Paso and was used to deserts. The gardener stood by listening, pruning the hell out of the last bougainvillea. He was a young man with massive shoulders and outsized hands, which the

Texan had no trouble imagining silhouetted against the white skin of his throat.

The night watchman must have been at least a hundred years old. He slept wrapped in blankets on the front porch. Every morning on the way to work the Texan tripped over him, had to kick the old man to get him to wake up. He wanted to fire the whole bunch of them, but the Americans insisted you couldn't be in Africa without a staff.

The first thing the Texan did was to reopen the rinderpest vaccination campaign. He traveled the northern steppe lands and savannas with two young Tanzanian graduates from the agricultural college, trying to convince the nomadic Masai to bring their cattle in for injections. One of the Tanzanian kids was sincere, serious about being a vet. The other wanted a desk, an air-conditioned office, training assignments to England or the United States. He didn't want to get dirty, pretended to get sick every time there was a field trip, leaving the Texan and the other kid to the dust and roadless stretches of Masailand. The Texan distributed zippers, mirrors, and toy scissors to the Masai. Women and children crowded around him, laughing at the way he tried to brush the flies from his face and out of his eyes, a fool at an impossible task. The Masai men were surly, and though the Texan tried to joke with them, they never laughed. Cattlemen jokes didn't translate well. The Texan's hollow laughter broke like gas bubbles, dispersed into the stirring sea of Masai cattle, orchestra of bellow, heave, and snort. Masai men took cigarettes from him and disposable lighters. They loved the cheap brass belt buckles. They asked him to bring them sunglasses the next time. But when he opened his vaccination centers, only a few Masai brought in their cattle. And those who came in didn't bring in all their cattle. They had a complicated fear of counting, part of it a fear of the government's taxes, part of it an old distrust of naming quantities. And they were all cattle rustlers, the young Tanzanian vet told the Texan. They had to keep their herds away from each other. Any gathering at a central place might bring a thief.

It bothered the Texan that though he traveled with the kid every day and thought they were friends, every night they separated. The kid would disappear to stay with friends. He seemed to have friends everywhere. And the Texan always had to stay alone in sad, empty hotels, painted in dark, garish enamels and smelling of kerosene. They served him boiled meat, boiled potatoes, boiled cabbage, and the salt and pepper tasted like moth-balls. Few white people traveled where he did, so at night he sat and watched the Tanzanian bureaucrats out on field trips. They all dressed like their president, drank the expensive warm beer, laughed their raucous black laughs, and turned their backs on him. Once in awhile, someone would try to make pleasant conversation, but after a short time the strain of English would begin to show and the Texan would be left by himself.

At home the Texan ate his sad, tasteless meals alone, served to him by the cook, who shuffled back and forth to the kitchen as though he were a stevedore lugging hundred-pound sacks. Then, for over an hour after those meals, the Texan listened to water running as the cook washed the few dishes, not more than a ten-minute job. Once the Texan stormed the kitchen, ready to catch the cook in some dishonesty, but he found the old man wringing out the dishrag to wipe the stove. He shouted, "What takes you so damned long to do seven dishes?" But the cook just looked at him, opened the dishrag, and draped it over the counter. He still hadn't put the utensils away.

Sometimes the Texan went to the tourist hotels in town for a meal. Sometimes in the bar he'd take up with lone couples who came in from New York, people who couldn't believe that a white man could actually *live* in such a place. Yeah-yeah, the animals were fantastic. They had seen it all: elephants, leopards, white rhinos, cheetahs, lions, the works. But the hotels were lousy, you couldn't get worse. There was nothing to do at night. And what could you buy? The souvenirs were crap. Ivory? The workmanship stank. India, they all said, was the place to go. Tourists who came in large groups didn't talk to the Texan at all, and on those nights the resident whores would come giggling, asking him to buy them beers, asking for cigarettes, suggesting they could be had for a pair of bluejeans, a pair of socks.

Pathetic whores. One wore a T-shirt that said EAT MY PUSSY. When the Texan asked her if she knew what it meant, she said no, she couldn't read, but she liked the picture, a kitten playing with a ball of yarn. She told him she was Ugandan, an orphan, her parents killed by Idi Amin. She had come into Tanzania over Lake Victoria on a fishing boat in the bottom of an oil drum full of Nile perch. She was very young and her small breasts were barely formed. Her hair was cropped like a boy's, close to a perfect oval skull, and her throat was slender like the women from the tribes who stretch their necks, a sign of great beauty. Her skin was much darker than the Texan liked, too dark, as black as her hair. It didn't look like skin at all, but like earthenware, made of the finest, the very blackest clay. It had a matte finish like Wedgwood, black Wedgwood. And there were no tones or hues in her face, no reds in her cheeks, no shadows under her eyes; even her lips were the same color. The palms of her hands. He was afraid when he kissed her lips that he would feel shivering winds of evil. He was sure she had come from hell. Her nipples were no blacker than the rest of her, all one color. And the folds of her labia like the fabled black rose. Clay—she lay there. With her eyes closed, she was pure jet, unbroken. He parted her legs with his hands, but there was nothing from hell, no raking winds of evil. She remained as pure as her blackness, unfathomable, untouchable, unreachable, impenetrable. She barely moved, flinched slightly as he withdrew, opened her eyes and asked him for a cigarette, his sperm shining on her leg like the slime of a slug's trail. He never touched an African woman after that. And the white, expatriate women were all married.

The Texan tried to open the idle cattle dips, but when the chemicals arrived he found the sacks had been rifled and filled with chalky dust. Like a detective he went after the thieves, checked everyone who handled the shipment right to the capital, to the top of the factory that produced the goods. It was a government factory— inviolable, unaccountable. A secretary looked at him blankly and said she didn't know where her boss had gone or when he would be back. Her desk was empty of everything but a teacup. She had no pen to write a message and borrowed one from the Texan. When he tried to reorder the chemicals he was told there was a shortage. There would be no more until the Danes supplied some. The Americans in the capital told him to submit a report, as his predecessor had always done, saying that the dips were operating. They didn't want Congress to find out that the project had failed.

At home in Arusha, the Texan picked up a German girl with a backpack. She was vague, traveling, on her way to India somehow. A boat was involved. She was meeting a friend in Zanzibar. When he brought her to his house, he was embarrassed by its emptiness. They ate the cook's awful food, waited drinking whiskey while the cook washed and washed the dishes, for hours it seemed, until the Texan went to the kitchen and shouted, "Finish it and *get out of here*, will you!"

In the mirror over his bureau he saw naked bodies like dead figures in a wax museum. The man was shrunken, bones and angles, marks of a tan to his biceps, dark on his neck, and a lurid torso. The woman was bigger than he, striped by a bikini. Her white ass and blond pubic hairs made his skin crawl. He wondered when he dropped her at the bus station the next morning if she slept with Africans, if she had given him a disease.

The Texan found out that there was anthrax on the steppe. And he found out that the Masai were selling their cattle for meat as soon as an animal showed the first signs of being sick. Worse yet, the dead animals were being left to contaminate the ground where they fell, while their owners scattered over the savanna so no one would know whose herd was infected. The lethal baccilli rested, waited, lived in the soil around the rotting carcasses for years and years and years. The Texan went in search of the disease and found it at a market in the blood-tinged, blue-black and frothing mucus membranes of an animal being hacked up and sold for food.

"Humans can die from that meat!" he shouted. Three warriors stood staring at him, decorated, handsome, lean as giraffes, their hair painted red with earth, plaited and falling to their waists. An old woman remembered him and asked him for a zipper. They didn't care. They didn't care if their cattle died, if their scrawny cows never gave any milk, if the roads and buildings that foreigners made for them lasted. They didn't care if their trucks and machines lay broken and rusting on the roadsides, halted, abandoned, returning to earth like the rotting carcasses of their dead livestock, sculptures of oblivion. They didn't care if they ate the contaminated meat of diseased cattle, drank the stringy, bloody milk of tuberculous cows. They didn't even brush the flies from their faces, out of their eyes, didn't care if they went blind from infections the insects carried on their feet. They didn't care if they all died. He wanted to seize the whole herd, the whole tribe, all diseased, and shoot them, burn them, plow the rancid ashes into a deep grave.

At night he stood near his table and threw his meal at the cook in damp handfuls. The meat was poisoned, he yelled. The cook stood fast and took the abuse as though, according to some strange code of etiquette, he shouldn't interrupt an angry white man. He gently retreated as the Texan's rage cooled. Later, the Texan heard him cleaning up the mess and the endless sounds of dishwashing until eleven thirty. The Texan checked his watch.

The Texan got tired of the way Africans pedaled their bicycles in the middle of the road as if they were the only damn people on it. To get them to move, you had to blow your horn at them and when that didn't work, you could come up behind them and nudge the bike with your fender. It shook them up; they'd wobble like circus clowns looking around behind, and inevitably they'd lose it, careen off the road into a ditch, twisted up and dirty, black and brown in the dust. Sometimes they'd just bounce off in front of his jeep and the Texan would have to stop fast. Once the Texan played his little game in front of the shocked, pretty wife of an American anthropologist who was supposed to study it up and tell everyone what the niggers were all about. She said nothing when the Texan, laughing his ass off, chased the bicycle. The African jumped off and ran around like a scared squirrel, and the pretty wife sat there silently, looking as though she had eaten something bad. But he could tell by the cold shoulders he started getting that she had spread the story. The Americans stopped inviting him to their cocktail hours and dinner parties. He was completely alone.

One Saturday night the Texan got drunk and, in spite, crashed an American party. They pretended they weren't surprised, pretended he had, in fact, been invited, asked him why he was so late. The hostess was drunk, too. She wanted to play her guitar and have a sing-along but no one knew any songs beyond the first lines. Near the table where they had put out the drinks and a cooler full of beer, the hostess took the Texan's hands and put them on her chest. She said she often thought of him living alone like that. Her breasts felt like foam, not flesh, and he squeezed them hard, too hard. She flinched in pain, pulled away from him, and asked him to go home. He bowed, grabbed a beer, and backed away from her out the door. He staggered to his jeep even though, by then, he was sober.

It was late and the Texan was surprised to see the man on the bicycle. His lights caught the form and lost it. It disappeared around a bend and appeared again in slow motion, almost still, as though neither one of them were moving. The Texan paced himself to match the bicycle's slow speed. His thwarted engine hammered like his quickening pulse. The man wore a white shirt. It was all the Texan could see, a ghost, the black head and arms dissolved in the night. There was only the shirt and a vague dark movement within it. The Texan moved closer, almost touching the bicycle. His headlights caught the head, turning now, and the red eyes like a terrified deer. The bicycle swerved away from the jeep and the white shirt seemed to crumble as though it had deflated. Then, as the Texan stepped on the gas to get away, the shirt filled again, there in the windshield, suddenly, like a stray balloon at a fair. The Texan felt the thud before he heard it, felt the wheels take the man, first one wheel and then the other as the Texan swerved in panic.

He thought no one was around. Breathless, he stopped: his head fell to the steering wheel. He smelled the beer that had spilled over his lap, spread like urine to the floor of the car. When he got out to check the body, a boy was looking at him, a freak with the fierce orange hair and colorless skin of an African albino. The Texan stared back. Fear had given the boy an erection, which he was trying to press down with his hands. It made the Texan laugh. He thought for a split second that he should also kill the albino, but instead he drove away. Police came the next day and the Texan faced the boy again. In the daylight the pink skin was splotched with ugly patches of brown, and the squinting, lashless eyes were watery.

The consular officer had to laugh. He told everyone that when he went to see the Texan in the gerzie, the cops had chained the cowboy's feet together. The consular officer got done calling the Texan an asshole; the Texan jumped up and tried to belt him one, but, of course, he tripped on the chain and fell over. You could not have much sympathy for the guy. The rest of the Americans in Arusha were breathing their sighs of relief that the cowpoke was no longer among their numbers. One of the women up there, a pretty little lady, the wife of some young anthropologist, said everyone had been worried about the Texan for a long time. She helped the consular officer get the Texan's stuff packed and out of the house.

The Texan's cook had meticulously emptied all the drawers and cabinets and organized the man's belongings carefully in carton-size piles. The shirts were meticulously pressed. The sheets were folded and tied with string. The half-empty bottles of shampoo and lotions were sealed in plastic bags.

"Nothing is missing," the cook told them. He told the consular officer and the anthropologist's wife that the Texan had been unhappy, he could see that, but that he was a good man and a fair man and the cook was sorry to see him go. "I have worked for Americans twenty years," the old man said proudly, "with no complaint."

Among the Texan's things, the consular officer reported, were some very strange items. A carton of zippers and cheap hand mirrors, maybe fifty of those little Jap sewing kits with the needles and thread, more of those toy scissors than you'd need for all the nursery schools in Chicago, and a box of metal belt buckles with airplanes and bucking broncos on them. It made you wonder.

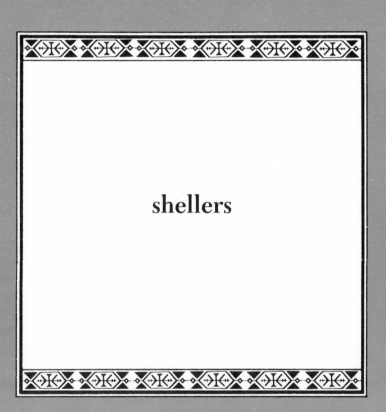

shellers

Paul had it all arranged. They flew south in a five-seater to Mtwara on the Mozambique border, so low over the sea that they could count white coral fingers on the stretching hands of reef. At the airport they shifted their gear into a waiting Land Rover. The driver took them east over a road washed beyond all definition and pocked with such deep holes that they feared their small ration of beer would be lost to its shattered bottles. Then they turned north following a sand trail to the sea.

First a village: low, brown, thatched, haphazard under heavy mango shade, its cluttered porches spilling into its muddy lanes, its people languid on stools and benches. They stirred at the sight of a car, only realizing after it had passed that the faces inside were white. Too late, children jumped up to chase the car as it bolted and skidded away. Next the green slope: banana and coconut plantations. Then the purple distance. Then the violet, the blue, the thin white stripe of foam where the waves broke on the beach.

Paul found the exact place with a hand-drawn map, a compass, several landmarks, and fifteen minutes of arguing with his wife, Erica. His eighteen-year-old brother, Danny, was silent, drowsy in the back seat. Long blond hair hung in limp coils over the boy's shoulders. His arms were thin and dry as dead branches. Those arms were at times all you could see. Gauges: changes when they came, showed here first—the gentle fleshing when Danny was well, the clear, moist skin, the color returned.

A final landmark fixed the spot. Six darkened oil drums in a neat row—weird black totems against the white sand. They were used, Paul had been told, by a local businessman who prepared sea slugs for the Chinese delicacy market. The man worked as shellers worked, on low tides, gathering animals from exposed reefs. Then he boiled them in his drums and dried them in the hot sun. Now the tide was high and the beach was empty. When the Land Rover stopped, they could see reefs under the deep water embracing the beach, dark green shadows like strong arms moving beneath fine silk. At low tide, they would be able to walk out to the corals and snorkel over them in search of cowrie shells. Paul Madison had one of the best collections of cowries in North America.

Erica, who worked for Pan Am, often joked that Paul had married her because of her job and the free tickets it gave them to the reefs of the world. This year: East Africa, following the moon and low tides along the mainland coasts and islands of the Indian Ocean. Paul had learned from another collector about this place—an undiscovered area, virtually untouched, virgin reef, rich in shells. On this reef, the other collector had found a very rare shell, *Cypraea beckii,* a tiny pale cowrie with faint blue and yellow spots over its surface. The marvel was that this was the first *beckii* to be found outside the waters of the Orient. The African species was so unusual that it had been questioned, but the find was verified and published in *The Journal of Malacology.* Paul had gone to see the collector and the shell in Boston and had returned home with the exact location of the find. He carried the directions like a map to buried treasure. In them was a description of the six oil-drum kettles of the sea-slug man. Paul wanted to bring up the second African *beckii.* Like Darwin, flexed with desire, he felt the wonder of life itself, the promise that his collection, laid out in the divided drawers of a cabinet, in stacks of boxes against the wall, numbered, catalogued, complete, like the pieces of a puzzle, would give him the answer to the mysteries of existence, to the secret of a species.

Squinting into palm trees, checking undergrowth, Paul argued with himself about which was the best campsite. He feared falling coconuts and the hiding places of snakes. Danny followed Erica to the water and stood behind her. Small colorless crabs rushed into their holes.

"So *beautiful!*" Erica said. Danny nodded, lips sealed. He had damaged teeth—a cracked and blackening mouth, lips held tightly over it. He rarely smiled. She left him there and walked slowly back to her husband. Above them all, the Land Rover's engine revved. Its tires crunched through dry, reedy grasses as it drove over the dunes. It would not return until four days had passed.

Danny had removed his shirt and flopped to the ground on his back, his bare belly turned toward the sun like a dead fish washed ashore. Erica slumped with the heat on the piles of their gear. And Paul was still pacing, testing the ground with his hands, checking the trees. They looked like people who had been marooned.

Effort and task thrown out of kilter in the heat, they pitched camp, slowly, wordlessly, dripping sweat on canvas. It was like doing a full day's work. They rewarded themselves with some beer, probably the last cold beer, Paul said, for four days. It was clear the ice they'd brought wouldn't last long.

Paul took his brother to the water then to teach him once again how to use a mask and snorkel. Danny did everything he was told without expression, his mouth a tight slit that didn't move. But he had trouble as usual, stood sputtering, pulling on the mask. Paul adjusted it for him, saw his face—the delicate, almost feminine

features, distorted, but more revealed—as a conun-
drum: the masked kid, eyes that accused. Or were they
hollow? Or were they seeking? The brothers dipped
again, bodies humped like sharks below the surface.
Then Danny seemed to catch on and swam ahead of Paul
for a while until, suddenly, he stood, removed the mask,
and ambled back toward the camp. Paul jumped from the
water and shouted, "DANNY!" in a rage, but the boy had
taken another beer and gone into his tent.

At night with lights and a full moon, they walked
along dead coral rocks that lined the living reef.
Mollusks, Paul told his brother, moved around at night to
feed on soft weeds and mosses. Cowries, especially,
hated the daylight. Their delicate external membranes,
called mantles, secreted the gloss and markings of the
shell. Light sensitive, sensitive to touch, if the animal is
disturbed at all, it will pull this skin away inside its shell,
like lips opening over teeth, exposing the dorsum, the
hard, egg-shaped exterior of the shell, drawing the
mantle inside itself through the slit in the base.

They reached a dark rock overhang and edged out
into weeds fallen with the tide. Things scudded as they
came, as their shoes sucked against the stones. Danny
pulled out ahead of them in the sour way he had of
making it clear that he didn't want to be with them even
though he had to keep turning, looking back, afraid to be
alone. After a while, he stopped and flashed his light
toward them. "Hey, Erica! Hey, Paul! Look! Look at this!"
They ran to him. Together their lights made a wide circle
over the mossy bed. It was a congregation of cowries
come to pasture in the night. *Cypraea tigris*, the tiger
cowrie, one of the largest and most common species—
the paperweight, the key chain. But here was a gathering
of forty or fifty of them. They were splendid, mantles out
like summer cloaks, fringed with white-tipped tentacles,

phosphorescent in the moon. Paul became excited, catching the spark from his brother.

"Hey, Danny! Hey, fabulous! Maybe you'll bring us good luck tomorrow. Shit, man . . . " He jostled the boy as he bent to pick up one of the mollusks. The delicate membrane withdrew; the spotted shell with leopard patterns gleamed in his hand, a red dorsal line brilliant. He gave the shell to Danny, "Here, man," he said, "you can start your own collection with this one. A real beauty." But the boy only shrugged, took the cowrie, and walked away from the crowd. He put it down alone and hunkered near it waiting for the mantle to slip out and over it again.

The beer was warmer each time they opened one, and they complained, ritually, laughing, because it tasted like rotgut that way. Paul decided to crack open some airplane brandy he'd bought, Remy Martin, and very good. Erica dug out the small snifters they had brought, a touch that pleased the couple in places like this and times like this, moon in the liquor, in the cradle of your hand, the cool shape of glass. Paul poured, then capped his bottle, then tucked it away. Sometimes she wished he wasn't always so—like that, as if they couldn't have all they wanted, even if they drank it all at once until it was gone. Sipping at things. They were silhouettes; their shadows, too.

"What color would you say that water is?" Danny asked. But no one said. He tossed his slug of the brandy down and waved his glass until Erica took it from him.

"God, it's great to get away," Paul said. "Well, Dan, did you ever think you'd be in Africa. Like this, just sitting on a beach in Africa? Drinking good brandy? And that moon?"

"Now, what am I supposed to say to that?" He looked at Erica. "Shit no, man," he said, "I *never* thought— wow—gee—me in Africa. I'm really here. Is that what I'm supposed to say? Oh, yeah, and that moon!"

"Don't ask me what you're supposed to say," Erica told him. She walked away toward the water. Jade, she was thinking. Black jade, if there's such a thing. The color of the water. Because the moon was yellow, drawing the slightest green out of it.

Paul said, "Okay, Dan, I'm not going to try. Forget it. I had this idea we might we able to talk, coming here, getting away. You don't have to say anything. But at least we can do things together. Meet me halfway on that."

"Yeah, okay," Danny said. "Sometimes it's better not to talk."

The voice contrite. Paul knows how Danny hates himself. How he lies on every occasion that suits him. Boys like Daniel are experts at it. No minimum self-esteem, they cover themselves with lies. The smart ones are best at it. Boys like this. Shrinks. Counselors. Years of it. Making progress, not making progress. Once Danny called Erica on the phone and talked about fucking her, talked about his hard prick, about her breasts, which he had taken the trouble to peep at more than once. Perhaps he needed to hit bottom and come up again, the shrinks said. Perhaps he needed to break. Until now you were sick of their clichés, their failures. Here, you take him now: we've done all we can.

In the morning they found the brandy down enough to notice and the bottle left out to make it clear.

"I don't think I'll be coming with you guys today," Danny said. "If that's okay." He grinned to show the worst of himself. "I'm a little under the weather. You know, tired."

"He's afraid of the water," Erica nagged, talking as though the boy weren't there. She regretted it, hated herself for it, her tone, but she couldn't stop. "He's tired. Tired of swimming, tired of breathing, tired of living! Well, I'm tired of him!" She threw her coffee on the ground and walked away to another dune, her breath heavy in her lungs from the heat, the humidity, the frustration.

They had to wait for the tide. Like a gambler dealing cards, Paul shuffled gear and put it out in three neat piles. Danny ate boiled eggs, one after the other, a magician plucking them from the air or from hens that lived in top hats. An old man appeared at the oil drums dragging sticks of wood in a big sack. He never looked at the campers, went on with his work, building fires under the kettles until the water in them began to simmer, rank with yesterday's catch. Then they watched him begin his strange harvest, shuffling toward the emerging reef, bent, looking down. Every once in a while he tossed something into his sack.

Danny, breaking suddenly from his lethargy, announced, "I think I'll go for a walk." He stretched, flashed a clown's grin, exposing his terrible teeth. "Issat okay?"

Paul told him, "I want you back in five minutes. You're coming with us." The boy seemed to acquiesce, nodded yes, then struck out, running toward the old man who was toiling on the beach.

"You can see how he looks," Erica said. "Horrible."

"But he's clean now. Look at his arms," Paul said. "He isn't lying this time."

"You'll never believe it's not your fault, will you?" she said. "It's no one's fault."

"That doesn't mean you sit back and let it happen," he said, "do nothing about anything."

Danny returned in the five minutes, looked at no one, picked up a banana, took the gear his brother had set out for him and carried it to his tent. When he came out, he was empty-handed, save for the banana peel, and his shoulders were squared. He was all stubborn refusal, heavy bones under thin flesh. He had very little body hair, like a child, but unlike a child's, his skin wasn't soft or supple: it was dry under his sweat. Paul grabbed him

by the neck and pushed him down through the low opening of the tent. Inside, Paul was yelling, hitting the boy.

Erica wept softly, weakly. When her husband
returned, she said, "It's always like this with him. Everything always ruined, always spoiled."

"He's staying in there, in the tent, doing fuck-all,"
Paul said, "hiding away like the creature he is."

The two of them alone carried their gear to the
water. Fragile living corals, green, blue, purple, fuchsia,
broke the surface like jewels. Among the outcrops and
the sheer sides of reef, Paul and Erica searched for
cowries. They swam first in the shallows with vivid fish.
They had to be wary of the poisonous creatures that lived
there on the reefs—stonefish, dragonfish, sting rays,
textile cones, fire corals, sea snakes. The equipment was
uncomfortable, the currents hard to fight, and the time
the tide allowed was compressed.

Erica watched Paul under the water, struggling
against his buoyancy, trying too hard to reach things he
had glimpsed in the coral but couldn't quite get. The arc
of his dive was graceful, but at the bottom he would
break apart into a turmoil of arms and legs as he
grabbed. She thought about the way he was on land. The
same. Even though here, under the surface, there were
no walls, and so many horizons. Even though the
vertical belonged to him.

Slowly the water rose and the reef gave in to it,
making it harder and harder for them to get down to
the places where the mollusks lived. When the tide was
too high, they swam back to the shore, taking it easy,
riding the waves, masks off and slung on their shoulders, propelled by flippers only, arms slack and resting
at their sides.

Paul had come up with two rare *Cypraea
contaminata*. He showed his pleasure by intently looking
at the shells as though they were gems and he a cautious

buyer. He held them, two tiny ovals, in his palm, pale blue-gray. Three dark bands like watercolor wash and a faint cloud of freckles glazed the rounded backs of the cowries. Underneath, on the base, was a rich, creamy white. Called *contaminata* because of the small shapeless blotch on the dorsum like a birthmark, a spoil. One of Paul's specimens was perfect. The other was flawed as though at some point in its development the crucial mantle had been damaged and the secretions irregular so that the highly polished surface of the shell was cracked and the pattern of dots and flushes was unevenly matched like a piece of china that had been cracked and badly repaired. Paul threw the damaged shell back into the sea. He fell flat on his back then, arms out, like a kid who will make an angel in the sand.

"We must be nuts to do this, to come all this way!" he said.

Erica was laughing. "For some old shells!" She dripped a castle of sand on his navel.

"How can it be," he asked her, "me and Danny? Our genes, our environment? I mean, we ought to be the same. Like those cowries. I had to throw one back. You tell me."

She said, "You're nothing alike. You don't even look alike." But there, lean, on his back in the sand, hair wet and flat against his skull, the eyes red from the water, the resemblance was strong.

They climbed the beach, weary and salted, and saw that Danny had not stayed in the tent. They met him and the sea-slug man busy at the kettles. Danny, with a home-made strainer, was lifting black lumps from the simmering water and spreading them out on the sand to dry. The old man was stirring. Up close, he was as wizened as his catch. His clothes were off and folded in a neat pile. He had a huge hernia that had dropped to his scrotum and was trussed up in a diaper that was filthy now from his hard work. Danny was that laughable red of a man who was going to suffer and peel.

"What? Did you finally get a job?" Paul's voice was harsh, angry, guttural.

Danny just looked at him. The sea-slug man spoke no English. The two of them were communicating, it seemed, in signs, odd words that meant nothing to either one of them, smiles and silences. There was, in fact, a pleasant rhythm to their task, stirring and straining, spreading the harvest—the bent ruptured black man and the tall, flaming boy.

Most of the second day, blistered and peeling, Danny spent with the old man. He rose before his brother and sister-in-law, started hot water for their coffee, boiled eggs, set out fruits and bread and butter. They saw him waiting by the kettles with a stick in the sand.

It was a good day for the shellers. Erica brought up a *mappa alga*, orange on the base, a southern African breed. And Paul, always one better, came up with *stolida*, a Mozambique variety, a flattened version of a shell he had found two years ago in the Philippines. But he was bothered, resentful, not speaking to Danny at all.

Before she slept, Erica said, "You're giving in to him: he's doing this to make you miserable and he's succeeding. Someday you'll finish with him and we'll all be happy. Mostly, Dan."

On the third morning it was the same. The breakfast was all laid out as if in spite and Danny was down near the kettles, a cigarette in his mouth, gathering sticks and dead palm fronds to start the fires. While Paul and Erica ate and waited for the tide to go out, Danny and the old man dragged their sacks to the water, heads back, laughing at something.

Erica said, "You bring him all this way. It's so damn expensive. He never wants to come. He hates to camp.

He hates to swim. He hates everything you want him to do. Why do we have to do this? What's the use of it?"

Paul answered, "We've come to find shells and we're finding shells."

Over the rock beds, soft black weeds like moss looked thin and dry under shallow water, but Danny's foot, pressing into them, found they were deep and slimy and he sprang back on a reflex seeking a clear surface, a patch of sand or rock. He hopped from that awful slime first to the left, stumbled, slipped, and caught himself on the right foot, arms extended for balance. As he stepped down, something hidden on the stone punctured his arch. It felt like a bee sting. At once his flesh thickened around the wound. The burn came fast. He saw the thing that stung him move away, a twang of a tail whipping powdery sand.

He thought he heard his brother calling, shouting at him for going barefoot on the reef against all warnings. He tried to stand still and wait for the pain to stop, to pretend it hadn't happened. But he couldn't. He had fallen, was trying to grab his foot now and rip it off. His strength was as enormous as his pain. He saw his foot breaking off in his hands. He saw it screaming like his own mouth where his heart had swelled. And then his leg, twisting it off, dropped from his body and he couldn't reach it, where his eyes were floating in icy tidal pools. An arctic sea. A boiling atomic sun. He was waiting for Paul to save him.

From the campsite, in the rise over the falling tide, Paul and Erica saw him fall. It was like a film clip, motion slowed as their understanding jelled. Danny stiffening. Danny crumbling. Danny grabbing and tearing at his foot, at his leg. and with the staccato images came the long howl. The old man rushed to him, looked toward the camp and back at the boy. Somehow, straining, he lifted the boy and carried him to dry sand. As Paul and Erica came, the old man broke away like someone afraid of blame. He moved faster than they thought possible, legs bowed around his enormous groin.

"He's stepped on something," Paul was yelling. "He's been bitten! Something's bitten him!"

"It's something bad, Paul," Erica said. "Is it really bad?" There was Danny's terrible howling and his body, compressed, churning, panting.

Paul said, "We'll move him to the tent. We can tie a tourniquet. I've got some adrenalin. I can inject him. Then I'll try that village. There may be a phone."

Somehow, struggling with Danny's weight and the flailing, they dragged him back, and Paul did all those things—the tourniquet, the adrenalin—while Erica whimpered and pleaded, "Dearest God, our Father. Please God. Please, Jesus. Oh, please, please don't let him die. Please help him, Lord. Lord Jesus. Make him well. Help us, please, Lord." She was kneeling then. Danny's eyes, which had been open in terror, had closed. His face had solidified. The screams seemed to come from his body itself. Erica was waiting for his exhaustion, praying and praying.

When Paul came back from the village, he told her, "There's nothing there. No phone. No cars. No busses for three days. No one can speak English. I tried to tell them what happened, tried to act it out. But they only laughed at me." He bent toward his brother. "Has the adrenalin helped at all? Dan? Danny? Good God, what was it?" He and Erica looked at each other and something awful passed between them. They wanted to leave, to go away and come back later and find him quiet at last. He was making too much noise.

Paul was close to the fallen boy, kneeling, first with his whisper, "Danny? Danny, can you hear me?" Then he seemed to collapse. Weeping, he tried to hold his brother's body. Erica was frightened. She had never seen him cry, never seen him give in.

"I want him dead," Paul whispered. He was sobbing

now. "To me he is already dead." He looked up at his wife. "I want him to die." He went on weeping. "Erica, do you hear what I'm saying. I want him dead."

She would have dropped down there to lie with them both, but the sea-slug man had come back. He was standing there shyly, frightened, twisting and twisting the rancid rag end of his truss. He was carrying a small leather pouch and gesturing, begging them to let him treat Danny. He showed them how he would make an incision on Danny's foot, how his poultice would draw out the poison, how Danny would sleep, how he would wake up with nothing but a sore leg.

"What is this? What does he want?" Paul ranted.

"He wants to help Danny," Erica said. Paul moved to grab the old man but she stopped him. "Let him try," she said. "They live here. They must know what to do."

He wanted them to light their camp stove and give him fresh water. In a small brass cup he mixed his medicine. Then he held his knife in the stove flame until the blade sizzled. He cut neatly across the ball of Danny's foot and applied the thick green paste. His hands were curiously small, the fingers stubbed, all the same length.

Almost immediately, Danny's crying relaxed. He began to moan. Slowly, it took hours, his body began to grow calm. The old man sat at a distance smoking cigarettes. Paul was pacing the beach like a sentry, passing the group at hourly intervals. Erica watched him as he turned to silhouette, to speck, then disappeared, and then returned in that order reversed. All night long his coming and going was like a pulse beat. From time to time, the old man checked and nodded, smiling, pleased with his work. He felt under Danny's arms and touched spots in Danny's neck like a doctor checking glands.

Though Erica thought it would have been impossible, she dozed, woke with her neck stiff on her arms. It was morning. Danny was asleep, breathing softly. The old man was gone. She could see her husband sitting in

the sand watching the sunrise, a strip of acid yellow burning far into the horizon. She walked along the beach to
him, cooling her feet in the water.

"Danny's sleeping," she said.

"I know," he answered.

"I'm not sure, but I think maybe he'll be okay. The
old man is gone."

Paul said, "You know, when we were kids—I was
twelve, so Danny must have been two—I hit him with a
toy truck, hard, really hard, again and again. They had
to take him to the hospital. Then they took me to a
shrink who asked me to draw a picture of my family. So I
did: with me and my mother off to one side and Danny
standing near my father's dead body. Funny, I remember it so well, being completely aware of what I was
drawing, doing it deliberately, putting it down that way
to goad the doctor. It made it easy for the doctor to say
what was wrong with me. He said I felt Danny was
responsible for my father's accident because he was
born the next day. The explanation seemed to satisfy
everyone. Everyone but me. Except that I felt wonder-
fully adult, as though I had reached their level and
tricked them at their own game."

Who would ever understand that sometimes violence was the only tenderness possible? But that there
had to be other reasons—anger or duty—to slap that
face, to touch that boiling skin, thin membrane, all that
was left of that poor flesh. Silence at dinner tables.
Sleeves clamped down firmly at the wrists. To hide the
tracks? Blue punctures in the green-white skin. And the
pupils? Dilated? The speech slurred? All of them bent by
his disgrace, staring down, wondering what they would
have to do. Did there have to be any other reason?

"Paul, say you didn't mean it," Erica whispered.
"What you said about wanting him to die. You didn't
mean it, did you?"

"No." He was holding something invisible that

wanted to crush his chest. "Not anymore." Was resignation the only kind of love he could offer now? To give in? To ask nothing? No logic to it. Not like the marked orders and suborders, the boxes and boxes of his shells. This strange love, born from his own helplessness. "I wanted him to stay that way. The way he was. Ruined like that. That's my secret. Wanted him to stay that way and never change." He was admitting it through the pressure of his throat, through whatever stung his eyes and this awful thing that was crushing his heart.

"What will you do now?" she asked him.

He got up and walked away then toward the sleeping figure at the camp. Bright birds on long red legs fled the path as he came, running just ahead of him until he started to run, too, and then they took flight, a flat solid plane rising and turning before breaking apart in the sky.

mama
angelina's

A man with a pale mustache is studying a piece of flattened brown paper containing a handful of stones. He moves one around and lifts it tentatively to the light. In front of him, transfixed, staring at his face for any sign, an African in a golf cap hunkers on bare feet.

"Yes, *ja*, they are diamonds, but useless, really useless. Maybe for industrial something. No-no, I don't take them." His accent is German.

Lydia has made her way across the veranda to sit between him and the woman she'd seen earlier, still at the same table, but now with a pot of tea. The baby she had been nursing then is now asleep, its head lolled over her arm. Behind her, a small girl, a child of mixed race, zips and unzips the woman's sundress.

"You have such a good baby." Lydia wants to talk to someone and they are strangers together here on a dull afternoon. Perhaps they are both waiting.

"This other one," the woman says, glancing behind her to the girl, "was never sleeping. I get nothing sleeping from this one." She has an East European accent.

"Well, they say the second one is easier!" Lydia is curious now, would like the diversion of a story—the brown child, the white one, that accent, in such a strange setting. But the woman is sluggish, her face puffed as if she has just awakened from a nap. It's the hottest, driest

163

weather of the year: a few ragged blossoms, plundered again and again by bees, cling to vines that cover the veranda. Now there are no leaves and the vines are choked into a dead netting. Lydia can see the driveway through it, slides her chair forward for a better view, listens for the sound of a motorcycle.

"Not so easy," the woman says. "You have children?"

"Yes. Two. A boy and a girl. But I left them at home in Dar es Salaam." Already, she thinks, I have said too much.

"You have a good *ayah* to watch them?"

"Very good. Like one of the family."

"Me, no." She looks down at her baby, who whimpers but doesn't wake, and wipes, with a loosened blouse, the perspiration from its head. "So hot," she says. "I am never getting accustomed."

"You come from a very cold place?"

"From Russia," she answers. "From Kiev. You know where is Kiev?" Her thin hair, turning gray, has been teased and molded into shape. She turns her head and the hair remains like a loose hat.

"I only know about chicken Kiev," Lydia joked.

"I would go back to Kiev. I have a paper to go back. It's there in the car." A man has entered as she was talking, growling and complaining that she has done something with his socks. He's an American and he nods at Lydia before he turns to the Russian and grabs her arm. She follows him then, lifting the sleeping baby to her chest.

Now there's only the sound of the German's laugh, saying no-no to the African. Lydia's watch tells her that Adam is late, more than twenty minutes, though it seems much longer to her because she had arrived far too early with an idea that she would be able to shower and wash her hair. It always looked best just freshly washed, deep auburn, curling over her shoulders. Her crowning glory, her mother used to say. One day, two days, and the curls were lost. But there was no water at the hotel. When she asked, she was given a plastic basin with less than a cup, to clean her face and hands after her long drive. It had disappointed her to put her fresh sundress on her sweaty body. She was damp everywhere, musty with her nerves.

The African in the golf cap is asking her now if she wants to buy his diamonds. They are real, he says, she can ask the *mzungu* sitting next to her, a man who knows these things.

"Oh, yes, they are real." He leans toward her. "But utterly useless. Even you can get much better synthetic ones." He tells the African, "Bwana, better you get diamonds from the diamond factory." He points to the pathetic stones. "Better you throw them away." The poor man looks confused. If they are diamonds, they are diamonds.

"They don't look like much to me," Lydia says. Pieces of soap, sea-washed glass. She shakes her head gently, no.

"Really, you don't get anything good here. I'm fed up with this place. But you are living here as well, no? I can tell."

"How can you tell?" She's amused.

He laughs. "Easy. You look so fed up, too. Don't you think you can stay somehow too long? I feel myself aging. Ten, fifteen years."

"How long have you been here?"

"Six months," he sighs.

"Looking for diamonds?"

"Minerals," he says. "I have a government contract from Germany. But it's hopeless, of course. Utterly useless. And this Mama Angelina's. Oh, ho! I will die in this hotel. So what is it you do in this place then?"

Always hard to answer—what I do is I accompany my husband, a diplomat, I take care of my kids—even harder now, so that she made up a story, "I'm a teacher at the American school."

"Before, I was living on tea and boiled potatoes

someplace called Saidia." He gestures to the north. "Do you know this word *saidia* in Kiswahili? It means 'help,' and that is a very good name for it too. HELP!" he shouts. "My wife was there. Now she goes back to Germany already. They give me a car and some equipments and every day I go to some village or other, to some office . . . "

It's as though his voice were drowning then, in the sound of the engine, in the dust it stirs. She can see Adam Reed through the tangle of vines, a series of broken movements and dark shapes, so tall he always looks awkward, adolescent. He takes off his helmet, shakes loose his long dark hair. He stretches, searches the grounds for her car.

Lydia has known Adam almost three years now, including a year of letters in the middle while he was back at his university hoping for another grant. Safe in envelopes, she sent messages that hinted at what they both knew. She wrote easily to him about an inner life in ways that surprised—images that rose freely, pictures of strange places, odd recollections as if she might have been someone else. I'm not the creature anyone really knows. Let me tell you, I can fly, see my long hair trailing furrows in the desert sand. We'll sit with Bedouins and drink their bitter tea that makes time die, your dark eyes and my dark eyes before us in a bowl.

His letters back to her were newsy and plain because he knew, of course, her husband Greg might read them. She could only feel between the lines what he might have said. He was alone, he wrote, tired of school, missing Africa. Finally he wrote to say that he had received the money and his research in Msangari could go on. There were dates and an arrival time.

He was a guest at her house as he had always been. He sat on the floor in front of her, pulling presents from a suitcase for her kids. When Greg went into the kitchen to mix their drinks, he ran his finger over her ankle and down the instep of her foot. He talked about the toy cars, the chocolate bars, a tiny doll, as the kids climbed over his back.

(Because he said once, long ago, I dreamt about your beautiful hair last night, and once, she saw, as she stretched to get a book for him from a high shelf, how he had looked at the skin of her waist, suddenly exposed, caught his eyes as she relaxed back. When he talked about his girlfriend at home—his "sweetheart"—she felt jealous and so she told him about the men she had known before Greg to make him jealous, too.)

That night when Greg was asleep, she found Adam in the garden. The jasmine was almost too heavy, embarrassing. He told her that he had kept all her letters. Then it was his dark beard burning on her neck, against her open blouse. He was falling. Here, let me lift you. She felt his teeth reach hers. There were long shadows as if the palms were pillars of a ruined city, an amber light, and they were running so fast their words were left behind.

Strangely, she was relieved when he left her house. Her letters to him went on and there were the phone calls on Wednesday afternoons, but her life took back its normal shape: the drowsy daytimes napping with her children, the wine she drank at night with Greg, his jazz collections and her operas. Lying in bed sometimes she was awake all night. This was her activity: eyes focused on pictures screened above her and flickering on the ceiling. These made her dreamy, even happy. Or words spoken softly to the dark. She wrote and told Adam everything she saw—paper umbrellas in an Oriental city, temples like the Aztecs', ladders to some high sacrifice, how they drifted in a green river, leaves, leaves all around them. She wrote and told him that someday she would come to be with him freely, dressed in silks that parted as she walked. And, honestly, she believed she would do it, when there was a chance, she told herself:

Greg on a business trip, the kids sorted out. Even as the opportunities came and went.

Now, let me call him. This time to tell him, yes, I'll be there. Tell me when, tell me where and what to do. He waits each Wednesday for her call at the mission in Msangari. At the bottom of the hills there, where the road ends, where there used to be a sisal plantation, is a hotel called Mama Angelina's. This time, yes. She was almost asleep. She could barely hear the night watch hailing a friend and voice like an echo returning the call. The old man was a shadow passing her window as he made his rounds.

Mama Angelina's was at the end of a curving driveway, down off the road. Luckily she saw the sign, had been warned how easy it was to miss the turn. BENVENUTO. ALBERGO. CUCINA ITALIANA. Adam told her the woman once was married to a Greek sisal baron. When he died, she stayed on and turned the place into a hotel. The building, a stone house in the center and a veranda, spread out in little numbered rooms constructed on falling fortunes, first brick, then tin sheets. The sinking porches were not on straight. There was a dog at the entrance hugely pregnant and repulsive, her turgid nipples and her mangy hair.

Inside it was surprisingly cool. Lydia looked around to see if Adam had arrived, but she was early, much earlier than they had planned, knew he was working. Heels clicked on a red tile floor. I am here. Hands vibrated from the long drive, holding the wheel in the heat, on the rutted road. Ironically, the cool inside released her sweat: it flowed in rills and soaked patterns into her dress.

When Mama Angelina came from the kitchen she had her head turned behind, owllike, issuing one last set of commands, first in Italian and then, as if providing subtitles, in Swahili. She was tied up in a mighty girdle so that only her bent legs moved as she walked. Her hair was blue-black, teased high, and wound in spirals and curls. She looked at Lydia and started to complain that her help was lousy, that she didn't have enough meat to make dinner, that there was no water, that onions were too expensive and her garlic supply almost gone, that her gardener had ripped up all her basil plants, that if anyone expected wine with the meal, they might as well forget it, and she ended up by saying that her daughter Mariella would show Lydia to a room, shouting, "MARIELLA! *Mo do' stai?* Mariella! *Wewe yupo wapi?* Where is you, MARI . . . ?" Like a tourist who has forgotten where she is and isn't sure which language to speak. When no one came, she raced off screaming, "MARIEEEEELLLLLA!"

The room was small with a single window close to the bed, and it smelled of kerosene they used to keep bugs down. The walls were turquoise and the floor red-painted cement, polished and polished to look like tiles. The iron bedstead, black; two wooden chairs and formica tabletop, all pink. The flimsy wardrobe seemed made of veneer alone, a shell. There were faded curtains, old kanga cloths, familiar patterns of cashew nut, yellow and brown.

Mariella, slack and sensual, a mulatto of fifteen or sixteen, leaned against the doorjamb waiting for her tip. Her hair took light from behind, plaited into four thick cornrows over her skull, a halo of red gold.

"Is there water?" Lydia asked. "Not even to wash these hands? See how dirty?" The girl shrugged.

Left alone, Lydia played with the furniture, moved the chairs, arranged bottles of wine, tried the bed. She unpacked, long soft sundresses, one each for two days and two nights, carefully selected from her most becoming. She understood, hanging them in the empty space, that her vanity was a shield she had put between herself and this man she would meet here, but she didn't know what to do about it. It seemed too late to change anything. A stranger, even to herself, alone with these unfurling clothes. Whose strands of red glass beads with their white hearts beat against her throat? Whose hair bound so tight it hurt, wet in the heat and slick, as though she had used dye or hacked it off?

She washed in the cup of water a boy in cut-off men's slacks brought to her. Like an Arab, she spread the moisture, a few oily drops, over her skin, then patted them away. Her astringent filled the room: she closed her eyes against its scent, against the wonderful cool of it on her face. When she pulled the curtain aside, she saw the kitchen yard strewn with cartons and broken clay pots, old rusting enamelware, bowls and pans, everything covered with the soot of charcoal stoves. The pregnant dog was there, lapping something from a dish. Under her tail, Lydia saw the animal was dilated, dripping, ready to give birth. She was swollen and worse, scarred and ulcerated where the tears of many litters had healed.

She tried to read, but the book she'd brought with her was as unfamiliar as her clothes. A page folded down. Have I been reading this? She didn't know. She turned back to the beginning and started again. And almost slept, stiff in the hard chair.

The little room fills quickly with Adam Reed. He spreads into the space. His shirt is off already, his shoes, as though he's shedding excess skin. Pieces scatter as he talks, on the table, near the wine bottles—a book, a notepad, pens.

"No water?" Well, he has hundreds of those airplane packets of violent paper towels. Freshettes. He uses one on Lydia, on her neck, on her shoulders, on the insides of her wrists, into her palms, down each finger.

"Your favorite wine!" she says. He's talking about what to do with her car, a plan; should they leave it and go up to Msangari on his bike, or take the car, try it over the terrible roads, worse in the drought than in the rains if that's possible.

She's laughing, "Oh, no—not my car!" sitting on the bed with her knees bent to her chin, her long skirt hung over her ankles. His things are flying, covering the room, a watch, a pocketknife, a visor cap. "No, no, have to go back tomorrow, after all," shaking her head. She pouts dramatically and lays her cheek against her knees. The cotton is soft, well washed, barely guardian to her flesh.

"Oh, I see." His eyes are still red from his dusty ride, his face too close, distorted.

"Yes," she whispers, like a vow. Did he really think she'd stay, leave her kids, face some kind of showdown with Greg?

"Well, then." He has his hand on her other cheek now, a rough contrast to the soothing cloth. "Well, I guess I'll have to regroup then."

She doesn't understand his tone or the changing way she feels, even with her eyes closed, trying to summon something, anything, but there's only her dampness and her desire to wash. He's trying to sit at the little table, but the small, crude chairs won't hold his frame so he paces, opening the wine, bringing her a glass with a toast, "To us." There beside her on the edge of the sorry bed. She can count the vertebrae of his thin back, touch his slender waist, the blades of his shoulders. Like that, until the first of the bottles is gone and her mouth is dry. She feels the stain of wine on her lips.

"You know," he says,—he has another full bottle of the wine, pressing it between her breasts—"we never talked about this, but do you . . . are you protected?" He sounds foolish, like a kid who's had a rubber in his pocket for weeks, waiting until his girl gives in. And she's embarrassed, feeling the wine as it deepens, as it reddens and drags her face away.

"Well, of course . . . " Embarrassed by the smell of her own sweat, stronger than his. If only she could leave right now, take the car with her favorite dresses folded up again, her secrets, in her bag. No wonder she's eager to drink more and more until she can't think or feel at all, nothing but her head back on the hard pillow and his hands pressing her shoulders and her own hands locked around his neck.

When she wakes there is no light, not even a sliver under the door. Pitch black. She moves slowly, sliding out from under her lover's arm, blind in the dark. Only the voices in the next room give a texture to the night, the American and the Russian arguing. The woman is weeping. Thump against the wall and then silence. There's his voice, muffled, as though he might be standing with his back toward Lydia.

The woman's voice answers clearly, whining, "But you have only to look. You see that he has your eyes, are green eyes. My eyes, brown." They seem to be moving furniture, perhaps to get at each other through the cluttered space. The thump again. Then Lydia hears a slap.

"I'm not stupid," the man says, very close now, as if he had come into Lydia's room. "Oh, God—how did I get into this?"

He slaps the woman again. She cries, "I go! I go back to Kiev! Let me go!" Sobbing.

"You can take your bastards with you." Something falls, a box, a chair. The little girl is crying now.

Eyes adjusting to the dark, Lydia finds the chair and table and drops, her cheek against her folded arms. Her hair is coming unbound, lank, filthy strands of it in her face. She has a headache from the wine.

"Tell her to shut up, will you," the man yells.

"Your son, your son," the woman repeats. "Who else? Who else?" Now more things fall, crash to the floor. "Look, look . . ." pleading, moving away and back toward the wall like a pulse. A light suddenly turns on over there and the dark around Lydia's room glows.

"Shut that fucking light. Because if you wake that

damn kid . . . " But the light stays. Behind the pattern of the faded curtains now, the fetal cashew pattern is given new life.

What if I should become pregnant? She imagines the torn bitch out there whelping in the terrible kitchen yard among the broken pots and char. At college, the girls shook bottles of 7-Up into their bodies or poached in hot baths. They drank a mixture of orange juice and castor oil, poured in layers. Here the women took massive doses of chloroquine and hemorrhaged. Her legs, which she protects from the sun, are parted and bare under her. She has nothing, on and it bothers her.

"Where is your mother?" It was Gran, heaped in her chair. You only saw her head, her hands and her feet, swollen and stuffed into pink slippers. They had put the blue stuff in her hair and the clouds over her eyes were called cataracts. Past the rows of tiny old ladies, the recital of their ages by nurses—ninety-four, ninety-five, ninety-seven, and Gran, ninety-two. They always left you to visit, perched on the bed, staring at Gran in silence.

"Where is your mother?"

"Out someplace talking to the nurse." A radio was playing what Gran called "dance music."

"Can you see her? Look carefully and tell me if you see her."

"I can't see her."

"Now come close. Stand very close to me and face that doorway. If you see her coming tap my shoulder, tap it hard. Do you see her now?"

"No."

"Listen hard, because I have to whisper. Here's a secret that isn't going to die with me."

"Don't talk like that, Gran." It was what you said to Gran, who was too old to die, your mother told you, too mean.

"Can you hear me,"—she dropped her voice—
"because I can't hear myself." Up close she smelled like
medicine coated with Noxema, the dark blue bottles at
her bedside, the ones that filled the trash bucket.

"Yes, I can hear."

"Are you watching the door?"

"She's not there."

"Listen, your mother had abortions, two of them. Do
you know what I'm talking about?"

"Yes, I think so."

"In my house. *My house.* We flushed them down the
toilet. I was the one who took care of her, told the lies.
You were three years old the first time. Then you were
five. Now how old are you? They were your brothers,
your sisters. Lydia, do you understand me?"

"My brothers. My sisters."

"Your *half*-brothers . . ." She was down farther in
her chair. You tried to lift her up: she was nothing but she
was heavy. The smell of Noxema could make you gag.
"You just remember what I've said and someday you'll
understand. She thinks it's all going to die with me."
Gran was slipping and there was nothing to grab: her
flesh came away from her like her dresses, layer after
layer. Gran's bones were crumbling, they told you,
breaking to pieces inside her.

The Russian's sobbing wakes her, but it's morning
and this time the sound is louder, as if the dawn has raised
the volume. Lydia meets her in the bathroom, staring at
herself in a corroded mirror, trying to arrange her dirty
hair somehow, but the pins won't hold.

She looks at Lydia in the mirror and says, "How can I
go back to Kiev? For me I like it and I go back. I am lawyer." Her mascara is dissolved, her eyes look tiny, a
mouse peering from smeared sockets. "But for my
babies, no."

"Are you married?" Lydia asks.

"No. Not married," she says and suddenly goes calm. With a comb she teases the thin hair and the pin finally holds. She tucks the ragged ends into a twist. This seems to satisfy her. No longer a hag, she wipes her eyes, normal again, and finds some lipstick. "He's so awful," she almost giggles. "I will never tell you how I am with him. I will never explain it." She looks amazed. She says, "I have marry a Tanzanian man—to get out of Soviet Union." She grins.

"Ah, you have a Tanzanian husband?"

She nods. "But he is no really a husband. I have bad lucks. Two babies. No husbands." She is placid now, amused by her own folly.

Lydia yawns. "I couldn't sleep last night."

"Because we yell."

"No."

"Well, I don't go back to Kiev, you know, because, you see, my children. For me is okay, for them is not okay. They can have no freedom there." Certain of it, she powders her unwashed face.

Lydia hesitates outside. Dirty: her feet, her hands, where her sweat has dried. She knows nothing has changed in the turquoise room. She wants to lift it, tip it upside down, and throw it all away, or else escape. She steps inside toward Adam, the long yellow column of his naked body, as if the surface of the floor were covered with glass, quietly, quietly, but she can't move without causing him to stir. He bolts awake, sitting up to see where he is, and then looks around for Lydia.

"Oh, there you are," as if he were certain she had gone. His black hair is wild, eyes swollen, lips thickened with the wine where his tongue finds the corners, facing her, his chest, his shoulders not symmetrical, the left side smaller, when she had thought him so perfect. The curtains lift with a breeze and reach to his arms, the cashews, obscene, stained there in yellow patterns.

"What are you looking at?" he says. He pulls the

sheet to cover himself and folds down with his back toward her to sleep some more.

In the end she refuses to think about any of it, to understand what has happened. If she remained dulled this way, she can say good-bye to him in the same tones she said good-bye to Gran that day with the deed sealed up inside. How many years was it before Gran died? She was ninety-eight and she never spoke about it again, so Lydia hoped it wasn't true even when she knew it was, screaming, I hate you, hate you, hate you, but never out loud. Leaning against her car, hearing the sound of the motorcycle as it grinds the slope, takes the road, accelerates, she thinks about staying at the hotel another day, the day she had originally planned for. Sit on the veranda, think of nothing. But she wants to bathe too much, to shower, to drench herself.

"Nice, huh?" The German from yesterday. "A ruby. Very beautiful . . . " His pale mustache is like a mistake, a light smudge on a page, something that hasn't printed with the rest of his image. He holds the purple stone in Lydia's face.

"Oh?" She takes the thing.

The diamond merchant in the golf cap sways between them.

"But, Bwana," the German says, "you ask too much for it. Make a new price." The merchant shakes his head. The ruby is dull, shapeless in Lydia's hand. "You cut it so," the German tells her, "then really you have something. Maybe you make a better price, eh, Bwana?"

A ruby. She would have tossed it aside if she had come across it on the ground.

"Yes, sure, a nice one." The haggling goes on. "But if they catch me with it, pwaaaaf . . . " He makes a slash across his neck. "No-no, too dangerous to take this chance for that big price. I take a big chance on a small price."

"Take this one." The man hands him another, a smaller one.

"Pah, no, this one is useless," the German says.

"What is your last price?"

"Five hundred. *Mia tano.*" This insults the African, who turns to ask Lydia if she will take the stone.

"No, not me." She smiles, but something in her wants the gem even as it burns into her hand.

"Ask this bwana," the man says. "He will tell you it is real."

"You know, Bwana," the German argues, "they are making rubies in machines in Europe. So cheap you can fill a cup with them for this price. And you don't see the difference."

"No, I don't want it," Lydia tells him, her hand open toward him. He takes it and goes away, his golf hat pulled over his eyes, his pocket full of gems, bare feet patting the ground.

The German mutters, "Tomorrow he will be back with some lower price."

"And the synthetic ones, the ones you fill your cup with?"

"Horrible things." He grins. "Totally useless."

"But you can't see the difference?"

"You *know* the difference. This is the point. When you see a real one under a microscope, you see inside of it something purple, maybe black like blood. This makes it, this flaw."

It's her own guilt now, masked like the beggar's stone, the way she's been cut, facets to break the light. Thinks she sees Gran again, holding the dreadful message in her hands, giving it over, something purple marked inside, or maybe, as the German has seen, black like blood.

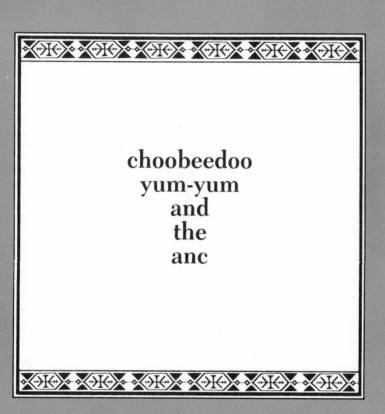

choobeedoo
yum-yum
and
the
anc

Patrick Nokwe, a South African, a Zulu brother, strolled in with someone the American had never seen before, a old man who was having trouble walking.

Nokwe said, "This is Jimmy, man. Just up from Mozambique. Jimmy, want you to meet the Yum-yum man here. Meet Choobeedoo." The Zulu's beard was wide, huge, with a tiny grin in there and worn-away teeth.

The old man tipped, fell as he sat. His face had a dusty gray on it, the remains of malaria or some other fever, fine as ash on the black skin. He leaned heavily over the table and asked, "Say, maan, you 'melican?" as though he would tear off the American's disguise—the hair pricked into an Afro, the dashiki, the beads, the elephant-hair bracelet, tire-tread sandals, mirrored sunglasses. But the old man's eyes were cloudy, fixed beyond. He was drunk, sunken, and he didn't really care. Nokwe poured him a tumbler of brandy—booze, glass, and all, pulled out of the Zulu's pocket.

"How about you, Yum-yum? A drink?"

The old man teetered toward the brandy and breathed, "Hey, baas, now what did you say that name is? Yum-yum? *Yum*? *Yum*?" He roared, spilling his sour breath. "You on the lam, 'melican? You running on the lam?"

The American smiled a little, shook a no, but this Jimmy would not let up.

"What is the story, 'melican?" He was trying to get his fist around the tumbler, trying to find it. "Tell me what. You know Stokely Carmichael?" He had the brandy now, was pouring it into his mouth. "I know Stokely. And I know Miriam. Miriam Makeba, Stokely's wife. Me and Miriam. Just like this . . . " He pressed two fingers together in the air. "We grew up. Same town. Me and Miriam." On a high note, he rolled into the American and then seemed to bounce away, stiff with a new idea. "Hey, maan," he said, "what about the story? I'm hearing that Stokely's gone back there. How can Stokely do that, maan?"

The bar was dark, tables outside under thatched umbrellas, tinny music and the smell of charcoal and kerosene smoke, the boiling maize meal from the squatter shacks out behind. You could see the car lights dip and flutter taking a ditch out there, lifting the broad yellow-green roof of banana leaf, layers to the black sky. Picking out shadows, a struck match. There were two men, one of them very tall, wearing a sports jacket even in the heat to let you know he had a gun strapped on his shoulder, a friend of Patrick's called Max. They were all guerrillas, training, waiting to go back to South Africa.

Jimmy greeted the tall man, trying to stand, while Patrick talked to the American about some British chick he had met at a party who had all the qualities he desired in a woman: blonde, able to speak English, married (very important), and driving a car (most important).

"I yearn for a fat bourgeois existence," he said. "A London suburb. Central heating. A woman cooking. I'd write my memoirs." Patrick had been an exile for fifteen years, most of them in Norway. "Max, now," he went on, "has a nice long Swede, an ex-model, husband always traveling on business. We try to stay away from women in the Movement." He laughed.

"Hey, where is the Movement?" The drunk surged, grabbing Patrick's word, pushing at the air around him.

"*Where*'melican? You know. You tell us." He reached for the American's arm.

"Nowhere," the American muttered. "Fucking nowhere."

"Who hands out the orders, maan? Chase Manhattan? Ford Motors? WHO?" He was yelling, standing up with his arms raised.

Patrick filled the glass again, tugging on the old man, urging him to sit down. They wanted him drunk, wanted him to pass out. The old man said something in their own language. It sounded urgent. Patrick translated: "He wants you to tell him, you know, about the Movement."

Yum-yum. A name an old girlfriend fixed on him. And man, she was *old* too, had a good ten years on him. Called him Willi-yum and then Willi-yum-yum, then just Yum-yum. And then someone later started the Choobeedoo thing. Who was it? One of his sparring partners? Names, never pinned on anything more than the jokes you could make about him. Choobeedoobeewah.

Morning light in his bedroom, face grinning in the mirror reminded him that he was as old now as she had been then and though it ain't s'posed to show on black folks, it shows on this one. He sucked in his sagging gut. His chest swelled and dropped, sad pectorals that frowned like the rest of him. The face had a naked look without sunglasses, lines near his eyes and spirals of gray starting in his curly hair, tight springs of steel. It was coming in kinky, this stuff like the real stuff, as if maybe in his old age he was going to turn into a real black man. Octaroon.

When he was ten years old he had been adopted by a white woman, Miss Elizabeth Powell, a single lady of single determination. Formally and legally he became her son, moved into her suburb, did her proud. He got the good grades, was elected student body president in his senior year, captain of the boxing team. All around

Big Bill Powell. He was well-fed, well-dressed, though he felt that he lived in her house as a boarder. Put-a-black-kid-where-your-mouth-is. He finished Northwestern, but when he got out, instead of doing what Mother Powell wanted, he started to box. She didn't like it, too violent, so she changed her will and cut the young man out. William Powell (Yum-oh-yeeum) back at square one: black, broke, and orphaned. But the kid lost too many fights and was punched right back into the system.

Dig the new career: Mr. William B. Powell, economist, in the foreign service of Your Uncle Sam, far away in Tanzania, Africa, out there helping poor backward black folks. Right up Ms. Powell's alley. Working for A Better World. In his leisure suit, his Gucci shoes, splashed with Old Spice and hosed down with Right Guard, caught in the morning mirror ready for his daytime act. See that, Lizzy P., you done awriiight.

Powell lived walking distance from his office in a flat at Yasmeena Mansions, a run-down building full of Indians who cooked on charcoal burners all over the landings. For all the good it ever did, Powell continually griped about the place. There were no air conditioners but the one in his bedroom. There was no security. The first week, he walked in on three burglars rifling through his suitcases while two more stood in front of the empty refrigerator looking for something to eat. The biggest one swung a machete over Powell's head. One thing: living at Yasmeena sure made you glad to go to work.

Trouble was that Mr. Powell didn't work. He went to the office, drank coffee, and hung out at the Xerox machine making copies, hoping it would eventually print out a paper that would tell him what to do. He blew most of his assignments because, when it came to putting something down on paper, he couldn't. He was blocked. Done. To the men above him he made excuses, to the secretaries, to anyone who would listen. He made excuses to himself.

"They want me to fail," he told Mrs. F., the director's much much better half, the good Cynthia, "so they can say, 'Look what happens when you give a job to a nigger.'" She kept telling him he had it all wrong.

"Look at Joseph," she would say. Joseph, your original token: like original sin, everyone else is going to pay for it forever. He did not want to look at Joseph.

Today he walked, head down, right past the girl at the switchboard, hoping to avoid all contact, embarrassed because yesterday he had blamed her when he couldn't find any information of food shortages. "No American is going to find anything out around here. You people don't trust us." He had waved a pencil at her.

But she saw him sneaking by. "Goodi morningi, Missitah Powelli," as if nothing had happened. The chick had the squeakiest voice in the kingdom of God, like someone had tied a string around her vocal cords. You seriously had to wonder what people thought when she peeped at them over the phone like a strangled chicken.

The whole place affected him. He hated the woman in the office next to his, Susan Homer, promoted from the ranks of clerk/typist to Admin, to hold the militant cunts at bay; your new token, showing all the signs of acute menopause, refusing to authorize anything, accusing Powell of mistakes. The sight of her looming at his desk made him go for an early coffee break and extend it. It made him morose enough to prefer the fetid atmosphere of Yasmeena, wrapped in a cloth like some flaccid chief who had eaten too much cassava. So much for whatever day it was. He could only hope it was Friday.

His girl friend, a whore named Asha, found him that way hours later and dragged him out. Starving, she said. The food shortage she knew about was the one in his refrigerator. She wiggled around, thin and jumpy. She looked ridiculous, a caricature of a Western trollop based on ideas from outdated fashion magazines. Her legs were skinny, calfless, and her stomach protruded, possibly remembering some childhood starvation, possibly working on an infestation of parasites. She had turned up in sunglasses with white plastic frames, heart shaped.

They ate at the New Africa Hotel, in a bar, where the ham-and-cheese sandwiches had no cheese, where the mustard was finished, the bread dry, inedible, adulterated, not even made with wheat flour. God, what was that taste? Chalk dust? Talcum powder? The beer was warm. Asha mixed hers with 7-Up.

"Look," she pointed. It was Patrick's friend, Max, a spear, leading the way to the bar. His Swede was behind him rattling car keys. Her hair was slick, straight, glistening white-blonde. She had no hips under her tight white jeans, no bra under a loose jersey, big tits resting on her rib cage. Asha nudged Yum-yum, pointed at the Swede, and made a face. She whispered something about the white woman's hair: "Did she get it from a disease?"

The air conditioner made terrible noises but the bar was hot, the air only trapped, harassed by the machine. Max talked about South Africa. He hated America for backing the regime. He leaned, the plaintiff, coming forward on his elbows over the table like a machine lunging out of gear. His mouth opened on a very red tongue, teeth that were stained. His gums were pale, deficient.

The Swede changed the subject. "I'm writing a memoir," she said. "I call it *I, A Model.* Because you are an object, you see. That is my message." She laughed. Max laughed. Powell laughed. Asha was asleep next to him on the plastic seat where he left her, where he knew she would wake up in a stew of her own juices.

Next day he went back to work, right in to see Joseph F., the director himself, to complain about the new man, Bob Wendall, because he and Wendall both seemed to have the same job. The only conclusion was that one of them had to be superfluous. Powell wanted the answer.

He hated Wendall, a small bald guy with a fringe of pale brown hair and a little Hitler mustache, a real prick who smelled like he showered in Aqua Velva.

"Bob Wendall is a good man," Joseph told him.

"Which one of us has the job?" Powell asked.

"We hoped you and Bob might work together." A characteristic Joseph non-answer designed to drive you up the wall.

"Wendall is taking over my work and leaving me with the shit." There was this pained look on old Joe's sorry face. It riled Powell: he stormed out as if the fight with Joseph was sufficient reason to leave. The receptionist squeaked something in his direction as he went, her voice so high you couldn't even tell what language she was speaking.

Outside he was free of it all. Along the road to the waterfront, he saw dhows stuck motionless on a wind-calm moment, simple, graceful shapes like kids' cutouts glued to blue paper. They looked ready to fall off the earth. Voices from below reached him, dickering Swahili wives. Then he saw the women, fluttering shapes in black capes, starlings picking over the catch. He went down among them and bought a fish with a parrot's beak, blue and green scales like a watercolor of the sea. When the fisherman cleaned and cut it, there was a smell of flowers. He took it home, fried half of it, and left the rest for Asha. Usually when she showed up, she was ravenous, just awake, ransacking his kitchen. He waited for her, tossed in an afternoon bed, a masochist with the air con turned off, and finally at dark heard her singing his name, Chooobeeeeeeee, as she climbed the stairs.

Asha. They say if you keep going to the same whore long enough, she'll give it free. But what if she's been holding out so long you don't want it anymore? Yum-yum Powell, here with no hard-on in sight, and Asha trying kinky things in the dark room. The air conditioner was on now, pushing their stale efforts around with its roar. But the girl smelled of fried fish and had zero imagination along those lines and the Yum-yum man is tired of trying. Tired of trying.

"Are you drunk?" she wanted to know. She looked particularly silly, having tried to produce an Afro out of hair too fine that grew unevenly in tufts. Her Dark Angel powder was not quite dark enough and her lipstick seemed to have turned blue.

"No, I'm not drunk," he said. "But let's go get that way." His costume that night turned out to be even worse than the whore's, a woolen ski cap pulled over his hair, a Hawaiian shirt, mirror shades. He tried not to look, but there he was in full length on his bedroom door, a stranger, someone you would never want to be seen with. Choobeedoobeewah.

They found Patrick and the gang at the usual table, as Colonel Makassy and his *Orchestre du Zaire*, red berets flattening their big hair, three-inch platforms and flaring white jeans, were winding down on something Powell recognized as Stevie Wonder. Patrick had cornered Max's Swede and was telling her, "If they want to turn this miserable hole into a real country, they should take all their money and hire a bunch of Boers."

Jimmy, rising like Lazarus, yelled, "BOERS! *Ja.* On the veld we were all the time getting along. They kept their distance. We kept our distance. On the treks."

"It's an old story the Boers tell," Max explained, "about how the country was unoccupied until they got there. Pure shit. Let's tell the new stories." He had taken the old man's hand.

"New stories?" Patrick put his arms back behind his head, all beard then. The gesture released his smell, the showers he had missed, the rancid clothes. "You mean about the drunks? Twenty years in exile and no one back there to care. Tell that story, Max. Tell it."

"You talk shit, man."

"Sharpeville was twenty fucking years ago, man."

"The Movement ain't dead," Jimmy moaned. He grabbed for Patrick's shoulders. "We gonna take it back down there. The factories and each worker, man. To be beautiful, maan."

Patrick shook the old man from him. "*Ja*, Jimmy, beautiful."

"The WORKERS!" Jimmy shouted, but he was alone. Even Max had turned away. His long torso curved toward the blonde, a thin arm like wrought iron went over her shoulder. Asha was reaching out to touch the white hair, but the blonde recoiled, staring at the African woman in confusion.

"Fourteen years, maan! Fourteen years." Jimmy was shaking now. "Hey, Yum-yum, you know about me? Fourteen years." His arm went around the American and the tears, uncontrollable, poured from his eyes.

Later they all drove round to Max's, down in the empty city, a building that looked like a packing crate, a long hall through a turmoil of offices to a back stairs. An old woman met them at the door. She was small with awkward braids and she went right to Jimmy, guiding him, hovering over him, sitting next to him as he collapsed on the couch there. She had a compress ready for his head, chattering at everyone, her mouth full of ill-fitting dentures. Powell looked at them through his dark lenses, thought of what she saw instead of his eyes, her own face instead, doubled back on itself, her wild grin.

"What happened to Jimmy, Mother?" he asked her. He knelt there in front of them, put a hand on the sleeping man's slumped shoulder.

"Jimmy ain't nothing but a colored man. Like you." A witch's face. Teeth rattled when she laughed.

"Wrong, Mother, I'm a black man."

"No, sir," she said. "I can tell by looking. Have you got a pass, boy? The pass will say. Where's your pass, kaffir?" It was too funny, except to him.

"No pass. I'm American. We're all black folks there." She didn't listen, stroked Jimmy's head. She could have been a ghost in his shadowy vision.

"If you think this heap Jimmy is my man, you must sure be a crazy one." She laughed. "Myself, I had a real black man."

"Tell me about Jimmy," he whispered. He was close enough to smell the carbolic soap she used and the starch in her clothes.

"Jimmy was a driver," she said. "Drivin' in and drivin' out." She looked to see if the American had understood her pun. "He had a yellow van. Bullets poured down on it like rain. He took that van 'cross rivers and swamps and deserts. Ten years he drove it. Through back alleys full of coppers. Jimmy took my man out in that van. Me, too. Patrick, too. Pharaoh was coming down," she chanted. "Soldiers of the Pharoah—you know the story—coming down. Well, the last man he took out was hisself. Van was at the bottom of a river. Four ones were dead inside it. That was too many years ago." She winked, slipped along the couch until she held the old man's head in her lap. "My name is Heaven," she said.

Powell was drunker than he thought. There was an empty glass in his hand, a taste of cheap brandy.

"Hey, what are you hiding behind them funny glasses, boy?"

Hiding his tears. Because he wept these days over nothing, like a person grieving, like a black woman facing her son's first jail sentence, her best boy, her smartest.

Asha had asked him one night not long ago, "Choobeedoo, why do you cry?"

He told her, "It's an allergy." She didn't know what an allergy was, cocked her head to look at him. Her hairdo made her seem astonished, spokes of it bound in slick black threads stuck straight up in awe. Ironically, the style became her, showed off the soft swell of nostrils, the rich shadings of her full lips, the tiny flat circle of her chin.

Hungover at dawn, he stood outside Yasmeena not wanting to go in. Someone, a madman, was painting the place with what must have been the leftovers from a factory that had gone out of business. The front wall was chartreuse with orange trim on the balconies and deep green trim on the windows. They had started with turquoise on the stairwells. Once Powell made it inside, he locked himself in, days and nights, trying to sleep, eating stale bread and catsup, all the food left in the place. A dead man in a monstrous sarcophagus.

Who knew how long he was in there? The mirror told him he had aged beyond all records. Methuselah. Until one day he heard a voice on the landing call, "William Powell!" It was Cynthia, Mrs. F., thumping up the stairs talking to him all the way. She wanted to know why he had not been to work, why he had taken the phone off the hook. Joseph had made comments. Everyone was worried. Powell stuck his chalky, vitamin-deficient face out the door. She had something in a pan covered with aluminum foil.

"Say, that cornbrayed?" He managed a joke.

"No, you fool." She smelled of roses, skin the color of oak leaves in the fall, a rich red-brown.

"Frahd chicken? Poke chops?"

"Oh, shut up, will you." She had to giggle at that pickaninny there on his knees to her, even as she cringed when she saw conditions in his living room, like someone facing the public toilet at Madison Square Garden on the night of a big fight.

"William Powell," she nagged, "you ought to be ashamed."

Of course it was fried chicken and fresh rolls and slices of cucumber thin as paper with vinegar and sugar, and she was already at the sink washing him a fork and knife so he could get at it fast, telling him he looked horrible, derelict, out of control. He would have locked himself in the can then, to arrest the tyranny, but his hunger was stronger than his will to collapse, so he ate her food, fearing it meant he had been captured as her slave.

"I've decided to quit," he told her. "You can tell Joseph for me. Maybe I'll change my name. It's not a real name anyway." He told her he would stay in Africa but on his own. He had good friends. He identified. He might take kids off the streets, teach them sports, a kind of inner-city savior transplanted in the Motherland. But she heard his self-mocking tone and that made her sad, downcast. Her face was a perfect oval with the hair plaited into a high crown, the head of a forlorn queen copied from the priceless bronzes of Benin. But instead, she had to perform as mother, trying to force a vitamin pill, to hold his head against her chest as he wept.

"Ride it out," she told him. Louisiana lady with beautiful wide vowels on her lips. "Rahd it out, Willyum. Joseph had to rahd it out."

Fuck, it pissed him off. "Listen, Mrs. F., you know what I think about your old man." Then he capitulated, in a rush. "No, no, it's not him. It's me. I can't do it. I can't write. I can't think. I'm done, really done this time."

"But you *can*," she insisted. "Your background demonstrates you can."

"Goddamn it, you sound like some goddamn honky schoolteacher training up niggers to be good white boys. My background? What kind of background? Ms. Powell? Lady, I was nothing in her house, in her town, in her school. They were all pretending I was there. But no one saw me."

She looked surprised, as though someone had tossed her a ball when her back was turned. There would be no easy way to spin around fast enough to catch it. "People have to break their chains," she said.

"Sweet Jesus!"

"And when you do,"—oh, she could say it, too, daughter of a preacher, in the tones of the Bible— "when you do, you will see the raw spots, yes, telling you where you have been, and in your anger and shame, you tie bandages to hide the marks and you do what you have to do."

"Praise the Lord!"

"Don't think you have a choice, Mr. Powell, because you do not. Now smart up."

"Tell Joseph I want him to fire me. I want the severance pay. You tell him that."

"You think it over, William Powell." She could pout, a regal pout. He could almost smile, down as he was. And she could melt like chocolate because they went deep, deeper than she would ever admit.

She said, "I will not do your talking for you. You tell Joseph yourself. But you think it over. Joseph was like you once, but he could see it. There was nothing else to do."

"There was something else." Only he couldn't tell her what, how he wanted to be an African, go with Max and Patrick, announce his exile, train with the guerrillas, fight for freedom in South Africa. He thought sometimes this was the one thing left he could do, but it scared him, so he lingered, hoping Joseph would kick him into making the decision. "Tell Joseph I want him to fire me," he repeated.

"Absolutely no," she answered.

He walked along a bridge that spanned a tidal swamp where weird mangrove roots tangled above the earth and groped toward the water's edge. He smelled the muck of low tide steaming in the sun and took the long way, slow, stripped to a T-shirt like any black man in the heat, only he was so light that people stared. On a corner, a man selling old comics and potatoes asked where he came from.

"America?" he said. Called him "Negro," as if they were a race apart.

He went to see Max. It didn't seem absurd or strained; they were casual as hell facing each other over a cluttered desk with coffee and cigarettes, grinning, talking about the world.

"I want to join the Movement," Powell said at last. "It's the obvious thing for me."

"What can you do?" Max wanted to know. He unlocked clamped hands. Long fingers went like spider legs through his hair.

Powell shrugged. "Photography," he said. "Economics." There were others moving around them, in and out, women mostly in battle fatigues. He liked the atmosphere, the intense people, the black skins.

"The best thing," Max told him, "is to stay where you are. We'll decide when we can use you."

It was a good feeling then, lifting the spinal cord, clearing the head, the handshake and the smile, even the long disordered hall, the tumble of offices, going outside as though you were different.

It made sense. Stay where you are. So Powell went to the office. The pretense with a purpose. The receptionist didn't say hello but giggled like a conspirator when she saw him, handed him a stack of mail. He managed the act for days until Patrick called him and said there was a job for him. He should come around to Max's after dark. A long wait in Yasmeena, playing solitaire and looking for messages in the cards, Tarot reader, numerologist, urging him to take his chance.

A light led him through the quiet offices where he saw a woman sleeping in front of a dismantled radio. She stirred as he passed. Upstairs the room was like a transit lounge, the way they were all sitting reading paperbacks and dozing in their chairs. Something left from supper was on the tables, more plates than people, though they still seemed to be a crowd.

Patrick embraced him. "We need your help, Yum-yum. It's Jimmy. We need to get him out of town."

"Take him north. Change towns every day or so." A man Powell had never met was talking.

"You've got a car no one knows," Max said. "We'll explain it later." But Powell had seen the newspapers and knew. There was trouble in the ANC; they were arresting each other and being thrown into Tanzanian jails. No one talked about why. And he knew the CIA watched them and the CIA knew who he was, knew his car.

The old woman, Heaven, had come into the room. "Suffer the little children to come unto me," she said.

She's mad, Powell thought. They're all mad. He was suddenly afraid of them, afraid to do what they wanted, suffocated in that crowded room, the close, rank sweat of Patrick Nokwe like ether. "Not unless you tell me everything," he told them.

"Someone's after Jimmy, that's all. A mistake. We need a little time to clear it," Patrick said. "That old man can't be put in a jail. Some of us owe him favors."

It wasn't enough; Powell needed to know the enemy, he needed to believe. "Jimmy's harmless." He rubbed his face. If he could wake up. If they would ask him for anything else. Anything. There was this nausea, this vertigo.

"Last man he took out was hisself. Five in the van and the waters rising," the old woman said.

"FOUR!" Patrick shouted, automatic, lifting his hand to strike her.

"FIVE!" she shouted back. "Counting Jimmy." Her voice dropped on the old man's name and the Zulu's hand stopped helplessly in the air over her head. The old woman and her insane teeth.

"You've got the wrong man," Powell said. "I can't do this."

"Look, man, you said you wanted to join us."

"But Jimmy is harmless. Who'd want to put a man

like that in jail? What is this? What do you guys really want?" Because he couldn't trust them in the end.

"Who is this *colored* boy?" The old woman sounded lucid suddenly, full of hate. And Powell was wounded, cringing, afraid of their eyes.

The only thing a man could do then was go back. Back to Yasmeena. Back to his office. Back to, "Oh, Missitah Powelli . . ." like chalk on a blackboard.

"Yessi?" he squeaked back. She giggled into the phone right into the ear of some poor bastard on the other end of the line.

Joseph got him on the interoffice line, calling him Bi-yull, telling him how he and Cynthia were so terribly worried about him. "If there's anything I can do, son, just let me know. Cynthia looks on you as one of the family, you know."

"Well, there is something," Powell said.

"Yes, son?"

"You can fire me. I want the severance pay."

"Is this a joke? You better come see me. . . ." As if he were really talking to his son.

"I'm not your son," Powell said.

Back to Yasmeena. Back to the office. Back to Asha. Nothing wanted to change. Asha came to him wearing leather knee boots as though she didn't know she lived five degrees from the equator. She got them from a friend who bought them from the German woman she worked for. Now Asha needed extra money from Powell to pay for the things, called it an "advance," making it seem she was on some kind of salary.

Powell almost made it through two whole weeks working busily on a graph. Lines and coordinates. Supplies and demands. Axes. A graph, shit, yes. But, say, what is this cat graphing? By the second Friday he has completely forgotten. It must have been the graph of diminishing returns. Joseph called him and wanted to know if the graph was done. Oh, yeah, oh, sure, man. Piles of Xeroxed sheets were there. One of them most certainly had to be it. "On Monday, Joe," he said. "I'll have it for you on Monday."

So he didn't go in on Monday. Or Tuesday. Or Wednesday. His phone rang endlessly until he didn't know what it was and picked it up on a reflex, a zombie saying hello.

"William? Why don't you answer your phone?" It was Cynthia. "I've been calling and calling. I'm coming right over." And in ten minutes she was there, staring at him in horror, telling him what he already knew. He looked bad, hideous, pale as a white man, ready to die. She wanted him to come live at her house, a prisoner.

"No, Cynthia, I'm not coming to live at your house. I'm all right. A little down. Some malaria. A flu. It's over now."

"Oh, William," she was sighing, all that Southern, mossy draped sighing of Mrs. F., to woo a man. "You've forgotten everything. Forgotten that I love you."

"Someone's gotta do it," he joked. She brought out his best, his only happy. "Like collecting trash and garbage, right? Someone's got to love the poor kid—no mother, no father, et cetera." She held his wrist as though she would take his pulse.

"I'm okay," he insisted. "A small fever. Probably the flu. Totally cured." He grabbed her hand.

"You prove it then," she said. "Prove you're okay."

"What you want me to do, ma'am?" he drawled. "Hundred pushups? How about if I box your old man?"

"No." She paused. "You come to our party tonight. Washed and shaved. You come." She particularly liked this wild idea.

"Oh, shit, Cynthia, no. A party, for Christ's sake."

"Yes, indeed," she said. "You never come to our affairs." She called them "affayahs." How could he resist? "My little granddaughter Ellie has just arrived. I want you two to get to know each other. If you don't come, I'll send Joseph after you."

"No, pull-ease," he begged. "I'll be there. I'll be there." He stroked a hand so fragrant it floated. "I promise."

"Word of honor?" Her hair was pulled back into a bun. Not straightened, just gathered, shining waves like ripples from a stone tossed into a pool radiating from the center of her gaze. He passed a hand over her head, the hair undulating under his palm.

Somehow he rallied. Washed. Shaved. William B. Powell. Silk shirt. Gold ring. Beige slacks. Latest book: *The Gulag Archipelago*. Latest hero: Steve Biko. Scotch: Dewar's. Arriving suitably late. Cynthia, of course, was radiant in a Nigerian caftan, talking to the ladies. "I finally found a girl to take care of little Ellie," he heard her say, "I'm too old for a child like that one!" Nodding, welcoming her guests. She would have gone on herding folks like that onto the patio but Powell caught her robe, pulled her away.

"Oh, William, my heavens. Well, it's a good thing you came," ushering him in on her arm. Waiters in white coats brought him drinks. For some reason he relaxed. Maybe it was the scotch. He talked to some dude from the U.N. and with very little effort made it seem he really did have a job. Involved. Concerned. He found it so easy to pretend again. Bandages on raw spots.

Later, when Cynthia took him in to meet Ellie, he saw a little girl as beautiful as she was, on a huge bed in a puff of pink flowered sheets, fat as a cupid, brown as a gingersnap, golden as caramel.

"This is your new Uncle Bill," Cynthia was saying.

But the child was shy and wouldn't look at him. She showed the strange man her doll, peered out from behind it at him. There were kisses and good-nights; then Cynthia rushed away from them, back to her guests. He lingered, smiling at the girl, embarrassed, a second not more, then turned and stepped carefully into the

hall. In front of him was the old woman, Heaven, fingering her crazy braids, a smile on her outsize teeth.

"These coloreds your people?" she said.

"Black," he said. "In America we're all black."
Trying to get away from her but she had his arm.

"Jimmy's gone," she said behind his back.

"What's it to me?" He turned and faced her without
wanting to. "Where is he?"

"Maybe with the Lord. Maybe in the other place."
She grabbed his belt and pulled herself close to him.
"Who are you, baas? You CIA?"

"No, I'm not fucking CIA." He was so much taller
than she was, towering over her. She was tiny, brittle,
spiked as an urchin.

"Jimmy died in the van. You know it," she said.

"Listen, I am not CIA." At least that much had to get
through to her. But she wasn't listening, scuffing away
from him to her chores, up from whatever circle in hell.

Then, to make him prove it, she was there at his car,
coy as a teenager, asking for a ride. "My name is Heaven,"
she informed him in case he had forgotten. Other than
that they didn't speak. Everything dissolved in the dark;
even the car felt like a kids' slide in an abandoned park.
To close his eyes, to leap off at the end, legs straight, arms
up. A dream.

He was walking toward the light behind the old
woman, the long corridor full of boxes and rags. He could
hear a typist working somewhere down there, deep in
the ANC. Everyone at Max's was surprised to see him,
especially dressed as he was. Patrick stood, wrapped in a
towel from his long overdue bath, the beard wet as oil.

"She says they got Jimmy," Powell muttered,
wondering if standing here meant he would turn himself
over to them so they could punish him.

Max, who didn't look up, said, "No one got Jimmy."

"Jimmy's dead," Patrick said.

"Dead?" Powell asked them.

"Say, what is this, man?" Patrick came toward him. "What is this game you play, man?"

"Who is he?" the old woman whined as if she knew.

"Why don't you just go?" Max said. "We understand." He looked up then: his eyes, his voice could write a man off so fast. But Powell didn't want to go. He wanted to say something, to tell them what it had been like for him so they would really understand. But he could only make excuses, about his foster homes, his white mother, about America, about being an exile in his own country. Like Jimmy, yes, talking and talking about ruin and exile and making no sense.

"I said, GET THE FUCK OUT!" Max shouted.

"How can he be dead?" Powell was straining now with the tears that overwhelmed him so easily, not tears from the strength of his feeling but from the weakness of his will.

"He killed himself," someone said. Then Patrick was shouting, "This is not a garden party, man. This is not a masquerade ball." He lunged, tore Powell's shirt open.

"Patrick!" Max stood and Patrick fell back. Powell wanted him to come on. Wanted the Zulu to attack him. He would have fought, but only a little. They were both too soft to fight, too old, but Powell would punch once or twice to make it look good and then let the man work him over.

"Patrick, you can leave now. Cool it, man. Don't waste your time." Then the tall man, like a marionette with the strings let go, collapsed in angles to his chair. His gun was there, partly covered by a cloth. "We had you wrong, Yum-yum," he told Powell. "We made a mistake." He swung his long legs into another chair, held up the gun, cocking it and pulling the trigger, its empty pinging like a coded message telling Powell to get out and never come back.

Outside the moon had disappeared. Behind a tree? Behind a house? Its light still filled the sky. So late. So tired. So wide awake. But the bars were closed. Asha would be down in her village sleeping. The Yum-yum man was dead. William Powell had been caught. There wasn't anything he wanted to do for either of those two. Except sleep. Maybe sleep. Yasmeena, however, looked like a practical joke, like the thing itself had insomnia. He turned away from it and drove on, listening to the dark moan of his car alone on the streets.

In the soft vibrations left around the house after the party, he stood at her front door. The guard knew him, let him ring and ring the bell until she came, yawning, wrapped in a blue velour robe, smelling of a bath.

"William, what can it be? Your shirt? What's happened?"

"I need a place to sleep," he said. "You know, like, Yasmeena keeps me awake. Worse than caffeine."

"Come on in." Worried. The nurse, offering hot chocolate, a cup of bouillon.

Yes. A hot drink. Wonderful idea. He said, "You'll explain to Joseph, won't you, why I can't go back there? I'll tell him, but you explain. Say whatever you think is right. Whatever he wants to hear."

She nodded, had seen it at last, the only triumph he might ever have.

"But what will you do, dear?" she asked him. "What on earth will you do?" Knowing it didn't matter seemed to excite her. She was trembling, someone who understood what was given and taken from men because she knew the Bible, after all.

"If I could stay here and look at you." He smiled, touching the skirt of her wonderful robe.

"Tonight, of course, it isn't so important to know. But morning will change everything."

"Yes, I know," he said. "Only don't leave me, okay?"

He stretched on a couch. "Don't leave me until I've gone to sleep."

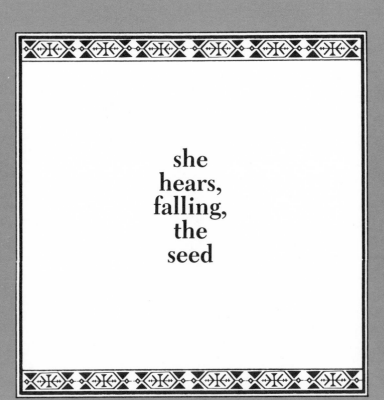

she
hears,
falling,
the
seed

. . . the walls, the gates, the dogs, the night watch-
man. There are wires to cut: telephone, siren alarm,
floodlights. All these things must be overcome.

In an instant the men are in the house. They pour
like floodwater, grabbing the lamps, the books, the
chairs, throwing them aside as they churn and roar. They
come crouched low and growling, curl back when they
see Emily, when they see Carl, form waves then and the
blades of their knives white crests.

Emily Frazier rose from her chair at the sound of the
breaking door. Now she watches as one of these men
comes at her as if he has torn loose from the surge, like a
rock and falling. She lifts her arms and sees him lift his. If
she is screaming, her voice is stifled in the racket. There
is only the tightness in her throat where the screams have
been. The noise of another man behind her stiffens her
spine. Already she is caving in on herself, blinded, as the
dull, fast footsteps come closer, close as the thud when
he hits her shoulders and she feels an arm at her throat
and another across her chest. She is being pulled down,
collapsing, sunk to the floor as if the sea had rolled and
dragged her under. She knows at once that terror will be
a kind of oblivion, without reason now, in total darkness,
struggling, swimming toward the surface, with her eyes,

her mouth shut tight, not breathing, fighting until she reaches the top, like a miracle, and breaks loose. Her lungs burst open and the air fills them. Away from him, from his hands that might have been claws down there where she has been.

"Let her go!" She has heard her husband's voice far away, now an echo in the rhythm of her breath.

And almost simultaneously the man who faces her is saying, "Let her go!" He could have been rescuing her, had taken her arm, was drawing her toward him. "*Mujinga*," he says, fool, and turns to kick the one who was slipping away behind her, a noise deep in his throat.

She focuses, counts five of them. They have smashed all the lamps. The only light is from the fire she and Carl had been enjoying, still soft, glowing, stealing the harsh edges from the details of the captured room. Five of them. One has his arm across Carl's chest, resting a machete blade over Carl's stomach. In the red light they both look corrupt, both held prisoner. The others pick at the room, opening cabinets and drawers, strewing the contents.

"What will you do to us?" Emily looks at the man who still holds her arm. She and Carl have been in Kenya so long, nineteen years, hearing about break-ins, preparing for them like fire drills, that the moment seems inevitable. And the face so easy to recognize. She can almost place him in a village on Lake Victoria, a Luo, black as obsidian, a high forehead, a wide jaw, prominent cheekbones. She knows the lanky boys and their broad-chested fathers who cut cane out there, has seen them whenever she went with Carl, an engineer, on his rounds of the sugar factories. Such gentle, serious people, she often said. But when they moved to the city, they lived in shacks made of cardboard and plastic bags down in the Mathare Valley. They changed. They drank *changaa*, spirits distilled from anything they could get.

He looks at her, squinting, an expression she had

often tried to duplicate, her "Luo-look," the smiling scowl. She is reminded of the faces of the young men whom Carl had trained over the years, their "African friends," they said when they went home to Wisconsin every other summer. Young men who sat intently at her table, picking at the food. Who never brought their wives.

> *They are Americans, the way she speaks. The man has white hair but good bones and a rich man's belly. Their women know ways to remain as young girls who have never given birth. They will put a color on their faces, a color on their hair. They will wear the clothes of young girls. In the same way, they close themselves inside their houses with lights to extend their days. In every house, the same rooms, filled with the same things. They will surrender their things to thieves because they are rich. They will simply buy more with the money they keep in safety inside banks. The safety they build around themselves, the way they know how to hide, this is what cannot be stolen.*

The men race with their blurring words around the room as they smash things—ashtrays, a glass of wine, the mirror on the mantle. Swahili too idiomatic, too fast for Emily to understand. The language wraps around the sound of breaking, splayed-out vowels and consonants that gather in anger.

"Where are my dogs?" she asks this Luo who holds her arm. "Carl . . . ? The dogs!" Knowing Carl is too cool to answer, stronger than she is. "They've killed the dogs," she cries.

"Emily, please," Carl says. He warns her with his eyes and his voice, so controlled it angers her. "Let them get on with what they're doing." She sees how pale he is, and his white hair, as if he had been made evanescent, as if he could trick these men and leave them holding his empty clothes, the blade against nothing but the air.

The Luo gives orders in Swahili. Tie the old man. Roll him inside that rug. Tie him there. This time she understands and knows that Carl does, too, although his face is still blank. And hers? which she doesn't seem to see at all even in her imagination, not able to see herself at all or find where she begins and ends. Only the pressure where the Luo holds her arm as if that were the last part of her left.

She watches as they tie her husband. His eyes tell her that he is offering her an example. Oh, she knows it all. Let them take whatever they want. Be silent. Give no way to anger. These rules. Old conversations return: her own voice saying, "Say nothing? Pretend they aren't there? Isn't that just what's wrong with the way we live?" And Carl: "Only the way folks lived about 1850 or so, J. P. Morgan, Pullman." He had theories about developing economies. What does he think now? Such a large man, so awkward to push him down even though he doesn't resist, rolled over and over until he's sealed away. He is the one out of danger now, out of their sight. She feels her anger, vague, heavy, spread in all directions.

She wants to call the Luo "bastard," or something worse, in Swahili but she can't think. She feels her breath against his face and wishes it were harsh, a substance that could scratch his skin. The others have already become voices at large in the house, in the rooms where her sons grew up, like echoes or even ghosts. Familiar sounds, drawers opening and closing, laughter, except that it feels like shame to imagine it, to see her clothes unfurled and strewn as the men press into the family's most private things.

"Where is the money hidden?" the Luo asks. He seems different, the way he doesn't care, the way he stays quiet while the others rampage.

"We don't keep money in the house," she says. She knows to make him wait, though they keep cash, two thousand shillings, in an antique chest to the left of the fireplace, ready for men like these who, everyone warned, grew furious when there was no money for them to carry away. Make him wait. So that he will finally be convinced that this is the treasure he has come for.

"You keep money," he says. He twists her arm. She could be acting a part in a play—rehearsed—all but the pain that she allows herself to endure, almost on his behalf, so that he will think he has won more than the cash if that's what he wants, to hurt her. All false, so that in her own gasp, she hears, falling, the seed of the violence that has brought them together like this. Her gasp, perfectly timed, then his release, a quick, sharp separation as a stem might split that has grown too fast.

"No money," she repeats. He takes her arm again, pushes her head down, harder and harder, until she says, "Yes, yes, over there."

Let go, she kneels at the chest, her back warmed by the fire. She removes the magazines, some sewing things, opens the lid. On top is the cash. She holds it out to him.

> *See how her eyes, the color of strong tea, tell the story. Always the money will be new from the bank, never touched, never folded. They will say, no, we have no money; then they will find it. Sometimes hidden in the house there is more. Sometimes not. There is no time to search. Word can go out, even when there is no alarm sounded. Someone will see, a maid, a child, and then they will call for help. The police will come suddenly. Then we must run.*
>
> *To come into this house, to take the arm of a woman like this. To see her eyes, to take all of these things, the money they offer. This gives no real result.*

He laughs. "So you have put it there for me?" Not taking it but moving in on her with his face the way he had done when he first entered the room, looming, his arms, like tentacles, were going to wind around her, going to crush her. She falls and crawls backward toward the fireplace. He comes after her, his black skin blushing in the light of the flames.

"You think I do not know about the rabbit garden?" he says.

"Yes, it is a rabbit garden, yes, yes, yes, but that's all there is," throwing it at his feet, twenty new, red hundred shilling notes.

"Yeah? Where is the real money?" But the others are returning. One is wearing two or three of Carl's jackets. Another has her camera. They have stuffed pillowcases but go on filling them, moving close to where the Luo is standing over her. They swoop down to gather the money from around his feet. As they bend, their machete blades flash like wings of wild birds around her head.

The Luo took nothing for himself and she loathes him for it, even though she knows he will get his share later. "What do you want?" she whispers. "What?" She stands up then so close to him that her face touches his. He doesn't answer, but, almost as if his heart against her own has said the word "everything," he reveals the dark secret she has been keeping—to give him everything, to have it over finally, as if she had conjured up that part of her nature that claimed to understand men like this. Or worse—looking into his eyes like a mirror—as if she, too, had been conjured from some part of his innermost being. It makes him the most dangerous because she isn't afraid of him, only afraid that she has been wrong and there will be no way to understand.

One of the others has found the liquor: he waves a bottle. They will get drunk, she thinks, and then what will they do? She wonders how long it will be before help comes, before there will be an alarm. Where was Ndolo, their night watchman? Where was Mumbi, their maid? Where were the dogs?

"Help will come," she says to argue them away. Her

voice, loud, threatening, surprises her. "You are not safe."

"We? Not safe?" the Luo says.

The one with the bottle goes to the phone and pulls it out, holding it in the air. She can't see his features, only the white T-shirt, disembodied, glowing in the dark, and the white phone aloft. "*Polisi hapana iko*," he says. "*Hakuna polisi.*" There are no police. The fire flares: she sees his arms, his face then like burnished metal.

The Luo is laughing. "*Piga Shaw. Shaw atakuja*," he says. Call Shaw. Shaw will come. The name enters the space like an eerie presence. Eerie as Shaw himself, the last white policeman left from the colonies. Emily has never seen him, only heard the name and the shock that goes with it when people of her kind talk about him— "jungle justice," they say—and the way, somehow, a man like Shaw is deserved in a place like this. As hideous as it is. As appalling as it is.

The men repeat, "*Piga Shaw!*" They laugh, rushing around in mock fear like actors in a comic battle.

> *We are such foolish men who laugh. Hah, Shaw, you are only a man. Too fat to walk without pain. Already there is a bullet inside you. If you fall, if you lie down, the bullet can move into your lungs and kill you. You drive all night in your white car to search for thief men. Inside, over your head, always a red light. When the car stops, the driver seat turns to face the street. Then you will lift yourself out by the strap there and the harness you wear.*
>
> *People tell stories about Shaw lifting himself in and out of his car. They laugh. But sometimes he will pass through the Mathare Valley in the night; the red light fills his car. Then everyone will look and say his name. Shaw. And then all the thieves will run to hide.*

The Luo says, "*Haraka.*" His word breaks over the laughter. Hurry. He pushes Emily into a chair and ties her feet with a rope he has taken from his pocket while the others go on scratching at the room, turning it over and over.

"Will you take things or only destroy them?" Emily asks him. He has her wrists and would tie them as well but stops suddenly and holds her hand to the light. The others are leaving, dragging their goods through the French doors into the garden.

"Your ring," he says. "Give it to me."

"My ring?" She shakes her head. It had been her father's, a heavy gold ring formed like a bird's claw and holding a small emerald. She wears it on her middle finger, never takes it off. To refuse him puts the ring at stake, not like the stash of hundred-shilling notes or the camera and radio covered by insurance.

"Yes, give it to me," he orders.

"No," she answers, "I will not." She is alone with him now. It's quiet. He is on his knees in front of her. "This ring comes from Ireland," she says. "It has a curse." It was a story her father had been told, that over the years had become a family joke: a curse, but no one knew what the curse was.

"An Irishman's curse?" He seems to think this is funny and turns the ring on her finger again and again.

"An Irishman's curse," she says. She has his interest, and his hand, which she had taken when it paused on her finger to handle the ring. "Don't take it," she whispers. She removes his hand but holds onto it. The hand is moist, muscular. He flips it over and grabs hers. She stares at the tangle they make, at her own pale flesh there waiting to be crushed.

"Irish witches?" He squeezes hard, hurting her, but she refuses to wince. "Give it to me," he says, releasing her hand and holding out his own, palm up, for the spoils.

"You must take it," she tells him. Her hand goes out to him then. She could have been a bride, but in reverse, stricken. Her blood sends fire to her face. "You take it," she orders, "if you dare." As if she were protected against the ring's loss, as if there really were a curse.

He laughs. "You think I am the kind of man who believes such things?"

"I don't care what you believe."

"You think I am a stupid man?"

"Take it, if you are not afraid." She would force him into it, knowing he would always be afraid of the thing. "Take it!"

Slowly he removes the ring. She closes her eyes, feels it slide over her knuckle, feels nerves respond the long way up her arm and over her chest. Her nipples are erect as if he had touched every part of her.

He tosses the ring—the emerald catching the firelight—and puts it on his smallest finger.

> *Run out into the night, away from this house, down into the ravine. There is a fence there. And woods to pass through. In the morning we will meet and take out the things we have stolen. In our dark houses made of cartons.*
>
> *We will see then how much of what we take is useless, like this ring with its Irishman curse. We have no film for the camera, no money to pay the shops that make the pictures. We have no electric for the radio. The music on their cassettes is not our music. We will see that the clothes we have taken do not fit. The jackets will be too big. The shoes will hurt our feet. It will be dangerous to sell the things right away. Someone might see, might tell the police.*
>
> *Better to wait, hiding everything away, selling slowly one-one at a time. But it is easy to forget what is there in the boxes in the corner. Taking these foolish things, what else is there to do?*

Emily's hands have been left free. She unties her legs and rushes to Carl, sobbing, "Are you all right? All right?" Straining to free him from the heavy mass, her hands exploding with the effort and the knots which seem to be alive, unyielding to her frenzy. Calm, calm, she tells herself, until she finally sees his eyes, his mouth, can see his relief. He could have been a figure emerging from a column of marble, still so pale and barely breathing until she unleashed the last coil around his chest and he gasps. She falls against him, kissing his face, his eyes, as he smoothes her hair, like young lovers checking to see if everything is real, this miracle of each other's flesh, until she thinks, It's coming too fast, this euphoria, this belief that it's over, and gives herself away to the suspicion that there is still a danger outside. It makes her stand up quickly.

She can hear Carl whisper, "Dear?" But she has left him, is roaming around the edges of the room the way the thieves had done. It feels so much like grief, picking at those broken things. She wants a shower. She wants to sleep. She doesn't want to know about the night watchman, or the maid, or the dogs. She hears her own whimper as if from far away.

Carl calls her. "Calm down. We're fine now, Emily." He has hold of her, seems to be pulling her down from the ceiling where she has risen to escape.

Suddenly there are lights flashing outside and sirens and a keening sound of Africans from the shacks along the road as they gather to see. Through the window, Emily looks at them, a classic row of black faces arranged around events like this. They would stare and sway slightly, prisoners of curiosity, even the children, stone faced and serious, who already know that no one is protected. All they can do is call for vengeance against the thieves.

Carl goes outside. Emily follows. She pauses at the door as if on the edge of a pier, then plunges into the night, which washes like cold water over her skin. Mumbi, her maid, is there in the doorway, wrapped in a blanket like a victim of a fire. She tells her story: how she escaped, how she ran to the neighbors. It took long and she was afraid. They tied Ndolo, the night watchman, his hands and his feet. His mouth. Perhaps he had been sleeping when they came in. Perhaps they hit him on the head. He was an old man. Who would do such things to an old man? The dogs were dead. Mumbi is excited and her Swahili rises and falls with it: her words long and drawn out, her tongue snapping with anger and pity and dismay.

Police have filled the compound. Their fierce lights break into the dark spaces. They run, following their own dogs. One looks like a businessman in a dark suit and tie, carrying a notepad. Emily can hear the static from a radio he has clipped at his waist. She sees he is a Luo, too, an irony that makes her bitter, not about what happened to her so much as about the man who has her ring, although the two things are now twisted in her mind as if a covenant has been signed in their exchange. He is the one, she sees, who means more to her than this officious man who has come too late to rescue them.

Carl goes down to him. She can see them both gesturing, looking back at the house. The man nods, traces patterns in the dust with his shoe. Ndolo, the night watchman, joins them. Carl puts his arm around the old man's shoulders, hunched in a circle there like athletes before a game. None of what has happened seems finished yet and she is still detached, holding by a thread.

The crowd of spectators has grown. She looks down on them as if on a forest from a distant hill. Small flares from matches struck to light their cigarettes appear to her as lanterns, moving through the trees, of people gathering far away. She has to fight to remember that she is not alone.

"*Mwizi!*" a voice is calling. "*Alikamatwa!*" The thief: he has been caught. The crowd breaks apart, excited, as if something dangerous has been thrown among them. They fan out. They seek the voice. He is down in the ravine. He has fallen from the fence. Fallen onto some sharp thing. A stick that is inside of him. Immediately Emily thinks of the ring.

She starts to run with them, lost to the movement of their legs and arms as if they all have become one. She is pushed on by the sound of their shouting, smells of smoke and dampness that cling to them. She is afraid of what they will do to him, the instant justice—stones, clubs, severed hands.

"Wait! Please wait!" she is yelling. "Don't move him. Wait until a doctor can move him. . . ." She can see the fence in the tossing flashlight beams where the crowd has stopped and is parting to let her through. She goes slowly then. Somewhere behind her, she can hear Carl calling, telling her to stop.

Down in the ravine she sees the Luo, bleeding badly. He has crawled away from the fence to hide in the lantana that grows there. Crushed, the lantana has released a spicy smell, warm in the cold air like sweetened breath. He is watching Emily. Now it is her face bearing down on his. Now she is the one to take his wrist, to hold it with both her hands.

> *The woman's face is hard as a man's, even though she weeps. The old people have said there is a curse on all their things. But how can we listen and believe?*
>
> *Lights from the police draw a crowd to this place. Movement along the fence. Faces and eyes. They will come carrying sticks and knives. The children will pick up stones.*
>
> *If a man like Shaw catches thief men this way, he will make us lie down in the road with our hands on the back of our heads, our arms bent like the wings of birds. He walks up and down along the row. He presses a gun at each man's head. Will it be you? Or you? he asks. Sometimes he kills just one or two of us. A woman like this white one will scream, will say no!*

*no! but we Africans say Shaw is good, because we are
tired of being robbed ourselves.*

"I made it up," she whispers, "there is no curse on
the ring." There would never be enough time for him to
say that he believes her. A light has stylized the planes of
his face, carved it to some universal form beyond whatever he is feeling. He is perfectly hidden behind it.

He shifts slightly and withdraws from her grip so
that she nearly topples into him, her hands left reaching
toward him and fluttering. "There is no curse"—the
word itself a whip—"no curse"—cracks over her bent
shoulders, over the knuckles of her hands, empty until
she feels something soft and warm that is his flesh and
then the cold, hard metal pressed into her palm.

second
rains

She joined the foreign service when she was very young. The pay was good. The travel was fun. She bought things, beautiful, exotic things. She took the things home and showed them to everyone. They envied her. She told everyone about the cocktail parties, the ambassadors, the important people. Once the president came to Bolivia. She pushed through the line at a reception and took his hand. "My name's Charlotte Renoir," she told him, "I'm one of your secretaries." He had laughed at her joke.

Charlotte was assigned to Vietnam during the first years of the war. She lived in Saigon and she liked it very much. There was a kind of spirit to the place. On weekends, Americans flew in military planes to soft, far-off beaches. The secretaries brought sandwiches and the men brought beer. Charlotte had stayed slim, she colored her hair; she had a certain sharp wit that men found attractive. Sometimes it was a soldier or an officer she met. Sometimes it was one of the guys from the office who had a wife and kids in Manila. Temporary men. She liked them that way. The war meant nothing to her; she never thought about it all. She was happy in Saigon.

After that she grew tired of moving. She was sent farther and farther away, to places where there was nothing for her. They always housed her in apartment buildings where the other secretaries lived. Other people at the post referred to them as "the single girls." She grew to resent it. She was typed, with carbons, clipped and filed like a report. She drank too much. She counted the days until her home leaves, the months until her retirement.

Charlotte Renoir kept herself up. People handed it to her. "That life must really agree with you, Char. You still look great," they said. Did they expect her to fall apart, ravished by tropical diseases and shot up in war? Amebic dysentery and malaria and bullets were occupational hazards. She had suffered them all, but it had been worth it. She was very well off. No one working as a secretary in the States ever made such money. In a few years she would retire fully pensioned. She owned a house in D.C. and collected rent on it. She had inherited her parents' house in Cleveland and she rented that as well. She had a stock portfolio. She wasn't worried about anything.

Charlotte Renoir was assigned to Ethiopia in late 1972. She looked it up in the encyclopedia where she saw pictures of people wrapped in white cloths leading camels around, and she remembered something an Italian engineer in Brazil had told her. "Where there is camel is no good country." She grumbled around about it at the office but everyone told her the climate was great. She counted the years until she would retire. She could stick it out.

An Ethiopian employee driving a white Chevrolet met her at the airport in Addis Ababa. He had her name written on a little piece of paper and asked three women before he got to her. Charlotte watched him placidly, with a raincoat over her arm. "Miss Charlotte?" he said politely, when he got to her. He drove her to an apartment building that she knew was full of other secretaries. There was a certain smell of perfume (duty free). Everything she needed had been put in her flat: a refrigerator, a stove, dishes, towels, pots, pans, sheets. So she'd feel right at home, no doubt. They had even hired a servant for her, a nervous man who told her right off the bat that he could cook French, Italian, and Chinese.

"Can you mix drinks?" she asked him.

Her new boss was a loud fat Southerner who called her Tchaalit. On her first day in the office he told her to call him Chuck. On her second day in the office he jolted her by wailing her name at the top of his lungs from behind his office door. It sounded like a kid who had his head stuck in the slats of a crib. He wanted her to bring him some coffee. She smelled something when she entered the room: the man drank.

Yes, yes. She would write his letters for him. She would draft and type his memos and send out his cables. She would buy presents for his wife. She would just about *be* that man. And he would get the pay. His voice shattered her work space and her life.

One day, one of Chuck's Ethiopian colleagues— his "pals" he called them—came to the office. "Ato Kassahun," the man said, "Kassahun Afewerk." He saw that Charlotte was new and he extended his hand. "Charlotte Renoir," she said. He had a stunning face. Later she would know it to be a Byzantine face of ancient proportions—the high-domed forehead, the long, straight nose, the aristocratic mouth, the graceful cheeks and the large, mystical eyes of an icon. His hair curled gray at his temples.

He came to the office many times. Then he asked Charlotte for dinner. In all the years that she had worked overseas, she had never gone out with what the State Department referred to as a "host country national." What her parents would have called "a foreigner." Once a Bolivian in a hotel tried to pick her up with the promise of a spectacular weekend on a boat someplace, but she had passed that one up. Somehow it had not been made clear who was paying for it. Charlotte prided herself on being a realist, on never giving in to dreams, and especially on never being caught in a dream. If you were caught in a dream, she thought, you could never use reason to figure out the end.

Charlotte Renoir stood in front of her mirror like a girl. She moved here and there to catch different lights. The silk dress from Madrid. The shoes from Rome. She looked good. In all the years abroad, she had only dated Americans—marines, army men, men who traveled in and out as consultants on government projects, a stray businessman or two; even once a senator (a quiet dinner, a quiet proposition, and the quiet pleasure of refusing). It would be so strange with this Ethiopian.

Kassahun. "My name means 'be a shade,'" he told her. They ate Ethiopian food in the traditional style, sitting around a large basket. They used their hands and the flat sour bread to scoop up the spicy stew and the bitter cheese. Hard, salty, delicious food. "It's our custom that I feed you," he said. He took a small piece of the bread, filled it with meat, and placed it in her mouth. She wanted to sleep with him. "My wife is dead. I'm not married. I want to tell you this right away, in case you might think badly of me. I have two sons, still quite young. Only five and seven. My sons are everything for me. Everything. I don't suppose you could understand."

After dinner, they went to dance at a posh tourist hotel where there was a Western-style band. Kassahun was stiff and awkward. He was tall, very tall. And he was thin, too thin; she could feel bones on his shoulders and his ribs against her chest. He held her close, but delicately. "You are very nice," he told her. "The women of my country are old too soon." She didn't know what to make of him.

She went out with him several times. Somehow, although none of their evenings were what she would have called fun, she enjoyed them. She felt calm, detached from her own life, something that was pinching her like shoes on swollen feet. She liked Kassahun's severe and dignified ways, his petulant sort of honesty. She thought perhaps his behavior was put on for her, but it seemed to protect them and it gave them something to share—the distance between them.

One night he surprised her by saying, "I'm clean. I don't have a disease. Americans believe all Africans have venereal disease. This isn't true." Apparently the time had come. Sleeping with Kassahun was like the rest of it. There was no fun, only this detached calm. He was not self-conscious or trying to prove anything about himself. He didn't know how to pretend, so she didn't bother to pretend either. The best nights they spent together were nights when there was no sex. Charlotte sat next to Kassahun on the bed and stroked his long thin back. They might stay awake all night like this. She had a sense of melting. She wondered if it were love. The idea that she might love this man caused her second thoughts. She questioned his motives; she questioned her own.

Finally he told her, "I want to marry you." And then he stammered out a truth he probably had not intended to tell. "But I'm doing this to protect my children. I want them to have an American mother." Charlotte was angry. She felt had. "I'm not asking you to take *me* to America. But the emperor is old. When he dies, things in Ethiopia will change. I'm thinking of my sons and how to get them out of here."

"Oh, for God's sake, Kassahun," she said, "what on earth will happen to this place? It hasn't changed for three thousand years!" It seemed the wildest proposition she had ever had. He had built it up so elaborately and ploddingly.

"If you married me, they would be yours. You could take them with you when you left Ethiopia. Not me. I would stay here."

"Are you mad?" Charlotte asked him. His body was hunched, deferential: he had wanted to make a deal, to make it seem that she would have something to gain.

"My brothers were slaughtered in 1961: an attempted coup. We're in the wrong tribe. How can you ever understand this place? Look, right now there's famine. No one is talking about it, but they all know. Your government knows, doesn't it?" She nodded, and he went on trying to convince her that the famine would bring the palace down, could bring the whole country down, and that she, Charlotte Renoir, owed something to his kids.

"You want me as an insurance policy against famines and coups, is that it?" She laughed. "How about fires and floods?"

"Yes," he admitted. "But it isn't for *me*." He thought that made a difference. He amazed her, awakened her, when she thought she knew it all.

Charlotte Renoir took his proposition home with her. In her most flippant tone, she told him she'd have to sleep on it. But she didn't sleep that night because her decision had already been made. It was madness, but three days later she told Kassahun that she would marry him.

Millie Brown, her neighbor, said, "Charlotte! You can't be serious about marrying this Ethiopian?"

Millie said, "But Charlotte, you'll get a man when you go home. You look great. Not like me; I'll be bald in five years."

Millie also said, "They might fire you. You'll lose your clearance. You'll lose part of your pension."

And Millie warned, "He's going to expect you to send his boys to school in the States. Oh, it's as plain as the nose on your face."

And she finally said, "How can you do it, marry the fate of this horrible country?"

It was silly but Charlotte got carried away with her wedding. She wore an Ethiopian dress. She served Ethiopian food and hired an Ethiopian band to play music. Chuck burst in with a few cases of commissary beer shouting "Whar's the little lady!" She even liked *him* that day. Perhaps the Americans thought she was a fool. "Gone native," was what they said about men who made such marriages. "Charlotte's gone native." Did the smug wives of those paunchy bureaucrats look at Kassahun, so slender, so beautiful, and wish they could be Charlotte for just one night? They were stiff with their good wishes, but they all seemed a little threatened by the magic of her dare.

Charlotte and Kassahun went on a wedding trip to Tigre Province, Kassahun's home. It was a spectacular desert of high, bare hills and dry, fragile fields. Evidence of famine was everywhere. Kassahun pointed to it in fear; it was tearing away the country. Charlotte looked on it as she had looked on the war in Vietnam; it had nothing to do with her. Kassahun and Charlotte went on muleback far into the dead lands of Tigre to Coptic churches carved into rock hillsides. In the dark, cool back of the churches, she was surprised by ancient frescoes, the faces of saints, Kassahun's face, his high holy forehead, his sacred mouth, his blessed eyes. She was moved by the paintings. She felt compelled, baptized, and confirmed.

When they returned to Addis Ababa, Charlotte Renoir moved into Kassahun's house. She was surprised to find out how much she liked being with his children, Tesfa and Haile. She called them Tim and Hank. They had their father's handsome features and deep, mystical eyes.

Charlotte became the mistress of an Ethiopian household. Servants performed every task. Some of the servants had servants. They all lived in the compound. Charlotte moved from her intense privacy into a bustling community. It was not, as all the Americans had predicted, ghastly. She did not get sick from dirty food or dirty hands. She was not treated with suspicion and hatred. She did not retreat into cold culture shock. She warmed. She seemed to bloom, as though nature had surprised her with some second rains, rains that came after the dry season had begun.

Although she kept her job, and her boss, Chuck, still called her Tchaalit, Charlotte Renoir was changing. It surprised her how easily she could turn after she had reached the point where no turnings could be expected. She spun, like a dancer, discovering she was limber, fluid, still had talent. She practiced new steps with a flare, stretching on the bar of new worries, new jobs, new love. The stiffness was pleasant. Unused bits of her sprang to life. She studied Amharic and each new phrase was a gift. She felt another language would give her another identity. The children called her *enat*, "mother." She worried that they were eating too many sweets. She was nervous that their teachers were not the very best. She planned things with Kassahun: building a house in the hills outside Addis, sending the boys to college in the States. Sometimes she wished she were already old with him, beyond the risk of loss, someplace where life was still comfortable, nearly over. They would be there, together. She wished this because they lived under the shadow of a feudal kingdom, an anachronism, something that couldn't last.

In February of 1974, the ancient empire of Abyssinia began to crumble. By September, the emperor, Haile Selassie, King of Kings, Conquering Lion of Judah, was deposed. There were executions. Blasting noises reverberated in the streets around them. Charlotte Renoir had learned her Amharic, she had settled her life and her dreams here in this ancient kingdom, but she was still an American. This strange history overtook her in the form of violence, catching her in her dream: the executions of their friends, the sharp sounds of guns at night, the police everywhere. She had no context, no way to respond, no way to face things. She could only turn to those humans closest to her now. Her love for them grew.

Charlotte read *Time*'s and *Newsweek*'s coverage of the Ethiopian coup as though it were happening someplace else. The junta was a group of young air force colonels. The newsmen called them "firebrands." Their banner was revolution, scientific socialism, Marxist Leninism. There were speeches and harangues croaked out in a harsh Amharic she didn't understand. Kassahun translated, using phrases like "broad masses," "progressive peoples," "workers and tillers."

"God, what does that all mean?" she asked him. He never satisfied her with an answer. She didn't care to read Marx and find out either. She preferred to forget it. The Ethiopians seemed glad that the emperor was finished, although they made strange wry jokes about the young men who had taken over and the hopeless situation they faced.

But Kassahun rarely laughed. "They will probably arrest me," he told her. He worked for the Ministry of Land Reform and his record was clean. He had, in fact, fought for some land reforms and jeopardized his status with the old regime, but the new leaders were not seeking justice. It seemed they wanted revenge. "Now is the time for you to take the boys and get out," he told her. She refused. She said they would not arrest him, but she was wrong. Kassahun was taken from his office and charged as an agent of the regime, of the bourgeoisie and world forces of oppression.

The Americans at her office sympathized with her to some extent. Some assured her it would blow over. Others looked at her with "I told you so," written on their faces. Chuck said, "Aw, it's just a bunch of commie shit, honey." He was the kindest of them all to her. He gave her leave, said she was working at home for him.

Charlotte's life was exceedingly strange. Her office was at the embassy, on American soil: there was the sex patter, the football scores, the griping about taxes, the root beer and hamburgers in the lunchroom. Her home was an Ethiopian compound filled with people waiting for the worst. When she went there she spoke another language. She ate another kind of food. It caused her to wonder who she was, something she had never done much of before. She found no answers; she only found a focus—Kassahun and her boys.

Charlotte Renoir passed an envelope full of American dollars around to the right hands. In this way, she got permission to visit her husband in jail. She knew he would be angry with her for remaining in the country, but she went anyway. She dressed in mourning, the fashion of the day. A black veil dropped night over the bright afternoon. She saw only dark shadows in the streets. Police, stiff forms, moving deliberately, carefully. Any false move and a person stood naked, exposed.

She was taken to see Kassahun. The prison was cold in the rain. Her husband stood there, ruined, his skin chalky and his face sunken. Only those magnificent eyes remained the same. He was wrapped in a thick sheet. Charlotte remembered the picture in her encyclopedia. "Where there is camel . . ." she whispered, blushing. It was her attempt at humor. Where did it come from when she was aching so?

"What?" he said. They were embarrassed facing each other. She had the sense that they were no longer married.

"Nothing, just something I remembered. It popped into my head because you look so . . . "

"I thought you would be gone by now. Why are you still here?"

"I want to stay," she told him. "Kassahun, this is my home now. I want to live here. You didn't bargain on this, did you? I want to be an Ethiopian. Listen to me." He was turning away in disgust. "I want to understand this. And *you*. And face this with you." She was a romantic. It was coming out. It explained her marriage. It explained why she stood here now in these Ethiopian clothes of death and misery.

"Fool!" he said. "What have you ever faced before?"

"Nothing before," she answered. "I was in Vietnam. There I saw nothing. But I see this." She was determined to stay.

"They will kill me," he told her. "The trials are a sham. You don't understand Ethiopians. Don't even try. We're not worth it. I warn you, get my sons out of here."

"When they kill you, I'll go. I'll believe you then." She wasn't sure she meant it. She didn't believe he was in danger.

For months Charlotte lived on a twisting cord of politics and intrigue. Erroneous reports. Rumors. There was a countercoup of some sort. She never understood what happened. She could hardly remember the names of the men who murdered the men who murdered the men. People told her that there were factions to the right of the junta. They told her there were factions to the left of the junta. On weekends the wives of Kassahun's friends called on her. They all wore black. Their jokes were replaced by horror stories. They told her to get out. She could always come back.

Charlotte resented this revolution that had cropped up in the middle of her life. She wondered what these ugly men in their ugly uniforms had to do with her, how they could tell her what to do? They howled for justice and revenge. They blamed America. How could it be America's fault? Did America care about them? She was an American, and she had had to look up the damned place in an encyclopedia. Her anger brought with it a desire to stand firm against the bastards, to prove her innocence and her strength.

"If you understood us," Woizero Marta, her closest friend, said, "you would have left already."

"Not yet," Charlotte told her. "Kassahun is still awaiting trial. And the city is calm. Why should I leave?"

But things changed. A kind of insanity, beyond anything Charlotte had ever dreamed of, fell on the city. It began with the formation of neighborhood surveillance forces. They were called *kabeles*, and their job was to dig out counterrevolutionaries. They held quick, final trials. Resistance to the *kabeles* brought on more killing. All this was called Red Terror and White Terror.

Charlotte asked Woizero Marta, "Whose side are we on?"

"I don't know," Marta told her. "I only know they are people with guns." Marta was in agony, unable to hold a teacup. She told Charlotte that the *kabeles* were killing children. Mostly young boys. Charlotte didn't believe it. But on her own street a twelve-year-old boy was shot down. They said he was found carrying counterrevolutionary documents. Charlotte had to believe this because she saw the dead boy. His grandmother died within ten hours.

Charlotte knew there would be trouble getting her boys out. She sat in the offices of the new regime with envelopes full of enormous bribes. The weak, dim, corrupt faces of the bureaucrats of a few years ago had been replaced by the arrogant faces of army men. Hard and bright, but still corrupt. She crawled, as corrupt as they. She bought passports and exit visas for her sons. She bought them with American money, the money of the imperialist oppressors.

She told no one about the plan except a young British consular officer named Randy who arranged for tickets on BOAC. She told Randy that she was afraid to face the airport. She had no way of being sure her bribes would hold up. The passports were probably forgeries. The man who forged them knew. She had held them for one week. She was afraid it had been too long.

Charlotte Renoir packed in haste, the haste of escape, a hostile creeping rush that maliciously lingered, refusing to pass. She didn't know whether to go to the airport early and wait there or to go late, leaving them no time to notice or suspect. She thought again of staying, keeping the boys inside the house, teaching them herself.

"Where are we going?" Haile asked.

"America," she said.

"When are we coming home?"

"When this revolution is over. I'm tired of all the noise."

"Over?"

"In time it has to be over," she said, smiling. Time. Her enemy. Her friend.

She was afraid at the airport. Soldiers lined the entrance. They looked strained and confused, bodies angled oddly, as if the guns were new limbs and they were small children just learning to use them. Charlotte wondered if her eyes were giving it all away, telling them everything. As she came near, one of the soldiers moved toward her. She jumped, tripped, just missed a fall. Her eyes were on the gun. She wondered if the thing would drop down to block her way. But the soldier only laughed at her stumble. The gun relaxed.

More soldiers filled the airport. All she saw were the black eyes, the eyes of icons. Automatically (she didn't know what power drove her) she handed over the passports. The tickets.

A voice said, "Where did you get these exit permits?"

"They are correct," she spoke Amharic.

"These are not your children. These are Ethiopian children." He spoke English.

"I am married to their father. They are my children. They are holding valid exit permits, issued by the ministry. The dates are clear." She relented, answered him in English.

"These are Ethiopian children" he repeated. "No Ethiopian children are permitted to leave the country."

"They are permitted. An exception has been made."

"An exception?" He stared at her. Perhaps he under-stood. Perhaps he wanted his cut. Charlotte had the envelope ready. Tesfa and Haile stood near her like stones. Were they still children? They seemed to have been pushed into old age.

"There are no exceptions," he said.

"There has been this one," she said.

"I will have to check it."

"There is no time," she said. He flipped casually through the passports, looking at her.

"How will you make it on time?" he whispered.

"Stamp them," Charlotte ordered, "stamp all of them." Numb. She opened her purse, found the enve-lope. Who? Whose hand pressed the money to him? His icy touch for an instant and the quick loud thuds of his stamp. Charlotte and the boys passed the guard. Then she began to tremble.

Charlotte Renoir flew with her children through hours of plastic trays and plastic food. The boys, excited, revived and grew young again, pushed buttons, twisted air valves, and drove their seats up and down. Haile peered out over the wing into the night.

"Ha! Enat, there is a fire on the wing," he said.

"Only the flames on the engine," she said. "It's nothing."

"Not going to burn the plane tzim! tzim! like the revolution?" said Tesfa.

"No," she assured them, but they were okay and not afraid at all.

"The fire is far away," Tesfa said. "It's a great wing!"

"Will they kill him?" Haile whispered.

"No. They won't," Charlotte said.

"But will they? Is that why we leave?"

"I don't know. Don't make me say."

"Then why do we go to America?" Tesfa asked.

"Because they are going to kill him," she said.

"Will they?" he asked again.

"Yes, yes, they will." The flame on the wing flared in the pitch.

Copyedited by Margaret Wolf.

Designed by Frank Lamacchia.

*Production by H. Dean Ragland,
  Cobb/Dunlop Publishers Services, Inc.*

Set in Caledonia by Compositors, Inc.

*Printed by the Maple-Vail Company on acid-free paper,
  and manufactured with sewn bindings.*